ME &
MR. JONES

LINDSAY MARIE
MILLER

And Cain talked with Abel his brother: and it came to pass, when they were in the field, that Cain rose up against Abel his brother, and slew him … the Lord saith unto him, Therefore whosoever slayeth Cain, vengeance shall be taken on him sevenfold. And the Lord set a mark upon Cain, lest any finding him should kill him.

Genesis 4:8, 15

Part I

The Golden Boy

Chapter 1

I saw him before he saw me. It was cold, wet, winter, actually, and I'd come to campus without a jacket or umbrella. He walked with a smoother stride than I ever had, up ahead on the brick pathway leading to the dining hall. It was college, so I could care less who saw me staring. There were too many people around for just one to remember.

Looking down at my sneakers, I followed the pathway, already embarrassed by the squishing sound I knew they would make once I entered the classroom. It was the first day of class since winter break. And even though I already had one semester under my belt, it felt like a curse to still be considered a freshman.

I had finally declared a major: Psychology. But once I learned of the experiments that we would have to not only conduct, but participate in, my introverted nature began to cringe. I was blatantly shy, and happily so, though the subtlest bit of focus in my direction made my cheeks blush scarlet red. It tended to bring attention to the sparsely scattered freckles at the apples of my cheeks and along the bridge of my nose. They matched the dark brown hue of my hair and eyes, no matter how finite the tiny dots seemed.

After sidestepping a few mud puddles, I looked up, and he was gone. I felt a strange surge of disappointment overwhelm me. Though I had lost nothing, it somehow felt that way.

In a hurry to make it to class on time, I skidded along the last section of the brick walkway leading to the psychology department. As I fell to the slick ground, the $200 textbook, that I had been nestling beneath my arms, slipped out from under them and came crashing down, into a soupy puddle of mud.

"NO!" I yelled aloud, devastated. All I could think about was that book.

Already on my knees, I leaned over the wet pool of rainwater and picked the book up by the edge of its front cover, because that was the only way I could manage to grasp it. But the book was too heavy to lift by its front cover, so the hardbound text slid from my fingers once again, returning to the puddle with a loud, offensive splash that coated my face with dark, tepid rainwater.

"You need some help?"

Just as I began to wipe the water from my face, I looked up, and there he was. The same tall, blonde, blue-eyed image of the perfect golden boy. He must have been a senior. I could tell that much from the mature bone structure of his face. He certainly didn't look eighteen.

"No, I'm fine," I murmured. My cheeks should have turned scarlet by now, surely, if not for the murky puddle drops on my face. Of all the days I had chosen not to bring an umbrella.

"Freshman?" He squatted down before me, balancing himself around the perimeter of the puddle.

"Yeah," I admitted, quickly averting my eyes from his.

He was dressed in formal clothing: a pale blue button-down shirt and navy slacks. I imagined him on the set of a fragrance commercial for Ralph Lauren, riding horses and drinking champagne. I watched him curiously, when he unbuttoned the sleeve around his right wrist and rolled the material up to his elbow.

He looked like he had lived in California.

He looked like he had been lifting very heavy weights.

He looked like he had outgrown this place a long time ago.

So what was he doing here?

Without a second's hesitation, he stuck his hand into the filthy water and grabbed my textbook. I snapped out of my daydream, practically in a daze when he motioned for me to follow him under the shelter that extended outward from the entrance to the psychology building.

"Open your bag," he requested, pointing to the

satchel over my shoulder. Once I did, he removed a brand new psychology textbook from the backpack he was carrying and placed it in my bag.

"What are you-?" I stopped myself at the sight of him shaking out my filthy, wet textbook under the dry shelter.

"You use mine, and I'll use yours," he offered, cracking a crooked smile. I shook my head in confusion, distracted by the crystal clear look of his blue eyes. They managed to reflect the tiniest bit of light, despite the lack of sun.

"But I-"

"You could just say thank you," he boldly suggested. I wasn't used to this.

"Thank you." I glanced down at the shiny new textbook in my bag, still in disbelief. He smiled, then walked towards the entrance to the psychology department. "Wait," I called, relieved when he stopped and looked back at me. "You're not a freshman. Are you?"

"No," he answered, holding my gaze, "I'm not."

"Well," I stalled, thinking of something else to say. I didn't want the conversation to end. "Why are you so dressed up?"

"I have a presentation," he said. His tone remained somber, professional even, despite the slightest hint of a playful smirk at the corner of his mouth. I wondered how often he looked at other girls like that.

"Oh," was all I could manage. I glanced down

at his shiny black dress shoes, doubting that they would squeak as loudly as my sneakers would once I entered the building. "Well, good luck." I gazed into his beautiful, clear, liquid blue eyes and admired the seamlessly sculptured face around them, in case I should never see him again. Surely, fate couldn't be so cruel, after being so kind.

"You too," he replied, before opening the glass door and stepping inside.

Once the image of him had vanished, I entered the building in search of a bathroom. Fortunately, I was able to dry off in there with no one else gawking at me. All the stalls were empty, and I was the only one at the sinks.

My first class was on the fourth floor, so I headed upstairs in search of room 481. When I reached that level, I found the classroom just around the corner, at the end of the hallway. Anxious with the first-day-back jitters, I opened the door and hurried inside. As the door slammed shut behind me, I noticed that I had come through the front entrance of the classroom, which meant that over a hundred people were now staring at me.

Thankfully, the classroom floor was covered in dingy, gray carpet, so my shoes didn't squeak as I searched for a seat among the crowd. There were only three seats left in the entire room, all of which were located on the front row, since that was the last place most students wanted to sit on a voluntary basis. Satisfied enough, I selected the seat in the middle and sat down between the only two chairs that remained vacant. Maybe I wouldn't have to make small talk with anyone this semester, so long as the empty seats remained empty. Just as I removed the textbook from my satchel and placed it on my desk, the thought vanished.

"Oh, did you get the book already?" a candid, feminine voice wondered. I looked up to find that the girl sitting to the left of the empty seat beside me had leaned over in curiosity.

She had a small face, green eyes, and a pile of light brown hair that she had pulled back into a messy ponytail. The ends of her hair looked a little damp, not unlike the collection of water spots on her t-shirt that appeared to be in the process of drying. I assumed that she must have forgotten an umbrella as well and immediately sought her ought as an ally.

"Yeah." I smiled, making my best attempt at polite conversation.

"Can I look at it?"

"Sure." I handed the heavy book to her. It was a fifth edition clinical psychology textbook, complete with diagrams and pull-out charts for studying.

"I heard it was really expensive." She flipped through the pages, briefly stopping when she came across a full color picture of Sigmund Freud. "How much did you get it for?"

"About two hundred," I replied, wondering if that was the actual price he had paid for it.

"That's ridiculous," she huffed. "I'm not paying that!"

I forced a laugh, only to be nice, really. Once our conversation ended, all was quiet again, so I turned around in my chair to search the classroom for familiar faces. I did not recognize a single soul.

When the door clicked open, I looked back to watch another student enter the classroom. A teenage boy with big glasses, dish water blonde tresses, and a sloppy posture walked in and sat down in the empty seat to my right. He kept his gaze down to avoid all eye contact, probably just as nervous as the rest of us were for the new semester.

Just as the door was about to swing shut, a dark shoe wedged its way through, catching the bottom of the door before it could close. When the door opened, I widened my eyes in surprise. I never would have dreamed that he would be standing in the doorway. Cool and confident, the golden boy entered the classroom, gracing me with his presence for the second time today. I immediately straightened up in my chair, anxiously anticipating him. The only remaining seat was the one next to mine, and I knew he would have to take it.

I cocked my head to the side when his feet moved in an unexpected direction, and he set his backpack down on the large desk at the front of the classroom. What was he doing?

Noticing me in the front row, he smiled in my direction, his blue eyes twinkling with delight.

Before I could comprehend what was going on, he opened his mouth and began.

"Hey guys," he greeted, waving a strong, manly hand in the air. "Welcome back. My name is Cabel Jones, and I'll be your instructor for this course. Any questions before we get started today?"

Chapter 2

After overcoming the initial shock of who he was, I could still feel the warm blood of my blushing cheeks, that had lingered there for the first half of class. Cabel seemed as down-to-earth as a professor could be in the eyes of a student, talking with an air of casual confidence. I was impressed to hear that he had attended college at Northwestern University, received his master's degree at Johns Hopkins University, and then finished off with a doctorate in clinical psychology at Cornell University. As if that were not enough, his desire for scholastic achievement was so great, that he had been able to do all of this on an accelerated fast track, meaning he was still only twenty-five years old.

With the presence of this newfound knowledge came a drastically altered opinion of him. He didn't look the same anymore, not at all like the charming young golden boy I had pictured him to be. Now, he was older, wiser, and more accomplished than any other man I had met of the same age. The planes of his face were harder, his cheekbones more narrowly defined, his jawline more taut and linear. I should have noticed that his shoulders were much too broad and muscular for a senior frat boy, who spent his nights juggling women and tequila. Cabel Jones was hardly like the narrative that I had conjured up in my mind.

In fact, he was bold, brilliant, and breathtaking. But he was also ineligible. The thought settled with me for a long time. Knowing that he wasn't a student only made me wonder how things would have gone that day in the rain, if he had been.

The following day, I stopped by his office, intent on returning the book to him. Mine was destroyed, and to keep his copy all semester just didn't feel right. So, when the moment arrived, I knocked on the partially cracked door to his office and looked inside.

"Come in," he called, removing a pair of reading glasses from his face. I approached his desk at a sluggish pace, pleased to find that his looks had not changed. If I hadn't known any better, I would have believed that he was the reincarnation of James Dean.

"Do you remember me?" My words sounded awfully meek, though I couldn't really help it.

"Ah, yes." He nodded, then set his reading glasses down beside a plethora of scattered documents on his desk. "The other day in the rain."

I kept quiet, remembering how embarrassing that day in the rain had been.

"Come in," he said. "Have a seat." I silently

obeyed, hoping that I appeared as cool and collected as he did. "So, what can I help you with today?"

I took a shallow breath, then looked down at all of the pages on his desk. They had been carefully spread out, like maps for a treasure hunt. What was he looking for?

"I wanted to give you your book back." I reached into my satchel and grabbed the heavy textbook. "I know it's expensive," I admitted, "and you shouldn't have to use the one that I dropped in the water." Pleased with myself, I handed the book over his desk and waited for him to take it. Despite my innocent smile, Cabel folded his hands together and relaxed into the back of his chair. He wasn't interested.

"I don't have your book," Cabel confessed.

"Oh." I wiped the smile off my face and returned the book to my satchel. Hopefully, he wouldn't be able to make out the disappointment in my eyes.

"I recycled it," he explained. "If you had tried to take it back to the store and exchange it for another, they wouldn't have taken it." I furrowed my brow, not understanding him. "Because of all the water damage," he continued, answering my unasked questions.

"Oh, I see." My fingers clutched the satchel in my lap, nervously tugging at the fabric. I knew that the respectable thing to do was to offer to pay for the book. But I didn't have $200 lying around to cover the cost. I kept my eyes on the front wooden paneling of his desk, as I tried to think of the best way to respond. Before I could, Cabel sensed my inner struggle and spoke again.

"The publisher always sends me a few extra textbooks for every class, and I gave you one of those." I looked into Cabel's clear, liquid blue eyes while he talked. He was so young. "So, feel free to keep it," he offered. "I usually hand them out to students anyway, so it's no problem." Cabel toyed with the arms of his reading glasses, momentarily distracting me.

"All right," I agreed with a smile. "Thank you, Professor. I mean, Mr. Jones, er, Dr. Jones? I mean..." I closed my eyes in embarrassment, running a hand through my dark locks to ease my bewilderment. My heart rate increased, as I contemplated whether or not I had just displayed a lack of respect towards the man who would be administering my final grade.

He merely chuckled. The deep timbre of his voice stirred something within me that miraculously cooled my blood, if only for an instant. "Cabel's fine," he insisted. "I'm not much older than most of you, so there's no need to act like it."

All I could manage was a perpetual nod, until he changed the subject.

"So, have you signed up for the first experiment yet?" He leaned forward, folding his hands over the surface of his desk. I imagined that in thirty years, he would continue to age gracefully, like Robert Redford or Paul Newman. I hoped the blonde wouldn't fade.

"Yes," I breathed. "Mine is at 9:30 a.m. on Friday."

"Good," he mentioned, nodding his head with approval. "We'll have six more after this one, so make sure you pay close attention. Will this be your first experiment?"

"Yes, do you know what it will be about?" I couldn't help wondering.

"The topics should be posted sometime today, but the first one is normally pretty mellow, as far as intensity is concerned. It shouldn't be anything to worry about." He pressed his lips together, forming a thin, fine line. "Now, you've taken the prerequisite for this course, correct?"

"Yeah, I took it last semester, in the fall. That's the only prerequisite for the course, right?"

"Yes." He put his reading glasses back on and picked up one of the documents from his desk. "But this is an upper-level course, so be prepared, because it's going to take a lot more time and work than your lower-level courses."

"Okay." I slipped my satchel over my shoulder and rose from the chair, ready to leave. "Well, thanks for your help." I headed for the door, slightly offended that he had denounced my capabilities as a student, simply because I was a freshman.

"What is your name?" he asked, while I

lingered in the doorway.

"Finley," I briefly announced, surprised that he had cared to ask.

"Finley?" His piercing blue eyes held my gaze, contemplating and watching.

"O'Connell. Finley O'Connell," I reiterated, merely for clarification's sake.

"Well, Miss O'Connell, I look forward to having you in my class this semester." He grabbed a pencil from a glass jar resting on his desk and returned to his work, noticeably unaffected. I silently turned away, not knowing what else to say.

"Oh, and Miss O'Connell?" he called after me, just as I placed my hand on the doorknob.

I looked back at him one last time, wondering how I would make it through the semester with a James Dean/Robert Redford/Paul Newman look-alike as my professor.

"Stay dry."

Chapter 3

When Friday morning came, I felt a rumbling of butterflies in my stomach, as I headed towards the psychology building for my first experiment. I was told to wait in the lobby on the third floor, where fifteen other students were already fidgeting in their chairs, anxious to have the experiment over. One by one, each of them was called away by a young woman with a clipboard, who politely led them down the corridor and out of my sight. Within no time, I was the only one left.

Jittery, I rose from my seat and paced the length of the room, looking through a pair of wide windows. I spotted a handful of students on the brick walkway, down below, shouting and giggling, as they hurried off to class.

"Finley O'Connell." The young woman with the clipboard appeared, pen in hand.

"Yes." I clutched the satchel that I had been carrying over my shoulder and turned around with a smile on my face. I was prepared to walk down that long corridor and finally know what they were going to do to me.

"I'm afraid that your experimenter wasn't able to make it today," the young woman said. I felt my brow furrow in confusion, as I watched her scribble something onto a small notepad, before tearing a strip of paper from it. "Here." She handed the note to me. "You're still receiving full credit for the experiment today. That's our policy when the experimenter doesn't show up." She glanced down at her clipboard again, and then checked my name off the lengthy list.

"Oh." I studied the note in my hand. She had written down the amount of credit that the experiment was worth, and then signed her initials beside it. "Well, thank you." I shrugged, feeling each wave of nervous energy slowly lift away.

By the time I made it to class, most of the students were already there, discussing the various experiments they had just participated in. I grabbed my chair in the front row and sat down, unable to keep from eavesdropping on all of the others.

"They made me put my hand in this box and then I had to hit this button," one girl said. "Most of the time it did nothing, but every now and then, it would shock my hand." I leaned back in my seat and angled my body towards her, so I could listen. "I hated it," she cringed.

"Didn't they tell you what they were going to do?" the guy beside her wondered.

"Not until right before," she replied. "They made me sign a disclaimer too."

"We all have to do that," he declared, taking a tone with her. "All I had to do was watch some video, and then they made me answer questions."

"That's it?" the girl whined, scowling in frustration. "Lucky! That's so not fair," she griped, forcing an incredibly loud sigh from her lips.

I turned around in my chair and sat up straight, looking down at the textbook on my desk. Despite what Cabel had told me, the experimenting process was not going to be as relaxed as I had originally thought. I certainly wasn't looking forward to having my pain threshold tested, should that be the topic I received.

Typically, experiment topics were posted with a brief description at least a few days before the experiment date. But the faculty had just passed a new rule, which allowed them to conduct experiments without the participants knowing which topics they would be selected for. This was supposed to increase the validity of each individual experiment, since there was no possible way to form any biases or predispositions beforehand. If no one knew the nature of the experiment, then how could the results be anything but accurate?

We had all begun an unexpected game of Russian roulette.

I just hoped that I wasn't the first to get the bullet.

* * *

That night, I stopped by the grocery store to pick up a few things for the apartment. I was running low on food and would need plenty to survive my dull, study-filled weekend. How I longed to be one of those college students who could party and drink without a care in the world, while their grades staggered and their inhibitions dissolved. Wasn't it fun to feel that free? I would never know, and for that reason, I had always told myself that all the fun was overrated.

As I trailed through the grocery store, my eyes glazed over a selection of exotic fruits, imported from Brazil. I shook my head at the obscene price for one package of sliced mango. These were obviously not the delicacies reserved for my budget, so I waltzed over to the dairy section in anticipation. Finally, something with mass appeal.

A family of four created a wall in front of me, slowing the pace of my hurried strides. My patience wore thin, while I followed their languid footsteps to the dairy section. Once they grabbed a few packages of cheese and left, I breathed a sigh of relief and scanned the shelves before me. A familiar face caught the corner of my eye, as I turned to find Cabel reaching for a carton of milk.

Panicking, I froze in place, then began walking backwards until I nearly collided with an elderly man on a motorized cart. "Sorry," I whispered to the man.

He looked me up and down, glaring as he

increased the speed of his motorized cart. "Teenagers," he huffed, then zipped away. You would have thought he was racing for NASCAR.

Thankfully, Cabel was still scanning the countless shelves of dairy items when I looked back at him. He hadn't noticed my scuffle with Jeff Gordon, so I still had time to make a break for it. As I turned on my heel, the family of four returned with their sloth-like pace. In a frenzy, I dodged the children, sidestepped a few soccer moms, and nearly collided with another cart-riding senior citizen, until I crashed into a display table, where an employee had just filled a tray with small, translucent cups of orange soda, to be handed out as free samples.

The table collapsed, barely missing the employee, as the samples toppled over, sending a wave of orange foam across the floor. I lay there, in a gushing river of cold soda, with the overturned table to my back. My hair and clothing were soaking wet, dripping from the sweet, carbonated beverage. I shut my eyes, exhaled, and tried to imagine a scenario that could have been more embarrassing. *Well*, I thought to myself, *you could have been naked.*

"Miss O'Connell?"

My eyes shot open in alarm. There he stood, the golden boy, towering over me with his beautiful blonde hair, light blue eyes, and muscle tone. Did he always look like he had just walked off the set of a movie? With the right lighting,

Cabel could have passed for a Brad Pitt body double.

"Mr. Jones," I squeaked, unable to hide my humiliation.

"Cabel," he corrected, offering an outstretched hand.

"Right." I placed my hand in his and let him pull me to my feet. "Thanks."

In a hurry to run and hide, I stepped around the orange stream of syrupy liquid. But the movement was a slippery one, as my shoes slid over the linoleum floor. Before I had the chance to fall, Cabel grabbed my waist and pulled me towards him. I felt his arms at the small of my back, supporting my shaky balance, while my hands found his shoulders.

"Are you okay?" he asked.

I nodded, feeling a sense of sadness wash over me, when he withdrew his arms.

"Here you go." The employee who had been serving samples of orange soda handed me a towel, and then dropped a yellow CAUTION sign onto the messy floor.

"Thank you." I took the towel from her and began the rushed process of drying off. "And I'm sorry," I added, just as she knelt down to wipe up the mess.

"It's okay." She smiled, then returned to her work.

Cabel grabbed my elbow and pulled me away from the scene, while I dried my hair off with the towel. We stopped to talk in the next aisle, where no one was handing out free samples.

"So tell me, Miss O'Connell," he chuckled. "Why is it that I can never seem to catch you out of the rain?" Immediately taking offense, I looked into his eyes and glared. Maybe Cabel was the pompous frat boy after all. He certainly looked it in his thin t-shirt and jeans.

"For a professor, you sure do act like a student," I boldly declared.

Cabel's mouth dropped open as he took a step back, unable to believe what I had just said. I could hardly believe it myself, but at least he knew what it felt like to be slighted now. I shook the rest of the orange liquid from my clothing and handed him the towel, which he quietly accepted. Frustrated, I ignored the disappointed look in his eyes and walked off, headed for the exit.

* * *

On Monday morning, I trudged to class with a sour expression on my face. I couldn't imagine what Cabel must think of me or what he was going to say. Why couldn't I be one of those students who skipped class every now and then? If I were, I wouldn't be worried about the look on Cabel's face when I walked through the door, because I would still be sleeping through my alarm. Why did I have to care so much?

When I reached the fourth floor of the psychology building, I spotted Cabel in the hallway and froze. He looked up at the sight of me and approached, as a sudden wave of nausea pulsed through my stomach. "Miss O'Connell," he summoned.

I lifted my head and looked up, into his piercing blue eyes. Cabel was wearing a white dress shirt with a black-and-blue striped tie, as well as a pair of black dress pants and shoes. I couldn't help thinking he looked handsome.

"Stop by my office after class," he instructed. "There's something we need to discuss."

I took a deep breath and nodded, but said nothing. Cabel opened the door to our classroom and let me inside, acting like a proper gentleman. Worry flooded through me as I made my way to the front row, because I knew what he wanted to talk about.

Why had I been so snippy at the grocery store? After all, he was my professor. Wasn't I supposed to treat him with the utmost respect? But that was just it. Cabel wasn't some sixty-five-year-old Nobel Laureate with tenure and an impending retirement. In fact, he wasn't much older than me. He had said so himself.

I avoided Cabel all throughout the lecture, too afraid to meet those light, icy blue eyes, afraid that he would be able to see into my soul, my fears, my past. When class was finished, I collected my things and left my seat in a hurry, already worrying about what he had planned for the two of us to discuss.

I headed downstairs and stayed in the main lobby for about ten minutes, not wanting to face the inevitable. What was he going to do? Kick me out of his class for being rude on Friday night? Surely, that couldn't be a rule. Could it?

Tired of stalling, I cast my fears aside and took the elevator up to Cabel's office, too shaky for the stairwell. When I arrived at his half-open door, I didn't even have to knock.

"Come in, Miss O'Connell," he beckoned.

Breathless, I swallowed my pride and walked into the room.

Chapter 4

Before taking a seat, I glanced around Cabel's office and observed how organized everything was. There was a wooden bookshelf that sat along the far right wall, whose books had been alphabetized according to separate categories and subsections of psychology. It looked like Cabel had an entire shelf dedicated to Freud and everything the man had ever researched.

His wooden desk was perfectly polished, clean, and devoid of the messy paperwork I had seen there last week. Cabel's framed diplomas hung on the wall behind him, just as straight as an arrow. Even the windows in his office were spotless, streak-free enough to fool a flying bird.

Why hadn't I noticed this before?

Curious, I sat down in the chair across from Cabel's desk and wondered just how often the term "neat freak" had been thrown his way. For years, I had heard much of the same.

"Well, Miss O'Connell," Cabel started, folding his hands over his desk. "I wanted to talk to you about-"

"I'm sorry, Mr. Jones," I interrupted. "I

shouldn't have been so rude at the grocery store." I shook my head and lowered my eyes to the floor. "I was just so embarrassed about falling down and making a fool out of myself, especially in front of you."

My cheeks flushed at the sound of my own words. What had I just said to him? *Especially in front of you?* Embarrassed, I bit my tongue and lifted my eyes to his face. To my surprise, Cabel looked just as lost as he was amused.

"Miss O'Connell, it's okay." Cabel levelled his eyes at me, turning soft, all of a sudden. "That's not why I called you in here today." I leaned back in the chair, unsure if I had heard him correctly.

"It's not?" My eyes darted from Cabel to his diplomas on the wall, and then back again.

"No." He shook his head from side to side, regarding me coolly.

"Then why did you?" I held his gaze and waited for him to scold me for interrupting, but he didn't. Instead, Cabel opened the top drawer of his desk and removed a thin yellow folder.

"So, David didn't show?" Cabel eyed me carefully, searching for truth.

"Who's David?" Was I in the Twilight Zone here? Nothing this man said made sense.

"Your experimenter," Cabel explained. "Last Friday?"

"Oh, yeah," I clarified, remembering. "But they still gave me the credit, so it's fine."

Cabel set the folder down, then leaned back in

his office chair. He placed his hands on the arms of the chair and looked at me. "Are you familiar with our new policy for experimentation?"

"Yes." I nodded. "We don't sign up for topics anymore. They are chosen at random."

"Right," he confirmed. "Now, I don't usually do this, but since you weren't able to participate in the first experiment, I will." Cabel opened the folder, collected a stapled set of papers, and handed them to me. "That's a list of all the experiments that need to be conducted this semester."

"Okay," I said, scanning the list before me. Apparently, these experiments were intended to test our limits, fears, emotional responses, and thought processes. It all seemed very standard to me. But I felt behind, now that I knew the rest of the class had completed at least one of these on the list, while I hadn't done any.

"Do you have any questions?" He leaned forward in his chair, anticipating me.

"Yes, I do." I rested the papers in my lap and gazed up at him. "What if the next experimenter doesn't show up again? I know that I'll receive the credit anyway, but I want to participate in these experiments. I want to earn the credit."

"I understand." Cabel angled his head towards me, a hidden smile straddling the edge of his lips. "I'll make sure that the next experimenter shows up," he promised. "David should know better, but I'll make sure you're placed with someone more reliable."

"Thanks." I smiled, feeling his eyes on me when I looked away. "And I am sorry," I apologized, "about last Friday." I shrugged my shoulders and stared at the ground. "There's really no excuse for it. I just wanted to apologize." When I dared to glance up at him, Cabel was smiling.

"You're shy, but only at first," he murmured.

His soft blue eyes traveled the length of my face, as I felt my cheeks blush on cue. When I widened my eyes at him, he pressed his lips together and smirked. The movement accentuated his pretty, pouty lips, though I wished it hadn't. I finally realized that having Cabel as eye candy for an entire semester of lectures was not going to be fun. This was torture.

"Thanks," I replied, not knowing what else to say. Before he could make a similar remark, I changed the subject. "I should go. My next class starts in twenty minutes." I rose from my seat and headed towards the door, but not without Cabel tacking on his two cents worth.

"Let me know if you have any problems with the next experimenter," he announced.

"Thanks, Mr. Jones." I had nearly reached the door, when he spoke again.

"When are you going to start calling me by my name?"

I stopped in my tracks and turned back to him, trying to decipher the tone of his voice. But Cabel's face had turned deadpan, expressionless.

Was he actually serious?

"That is your name," I boasted.

Cabel squared his shoulders, and then rose from his desk, clearly displeased. When he walked over to me, I felt my heartbeat escalate and my cheeks burn crimson. Cabel opened the door to his office, while I remained frozen in place, utterly perplexed by his behavior.

"Go to class," he commanded, motioning into the empty hallway. "You'll be late."

Darting my eyes to the floor, I walked out of his office and down the hall. The door slammed shut behind me, as I wondered what I had done wrong this time. Wasn't Cabel my professor? Wasn't I supposed to call him Mister? Besides, it wasn't like he had much room to talk. What was the purpose of calling me Miss O'Connell?

* * *

A couple of weeks later, I was due for the second experiment, though it was really my first. As I waited in the third floor lobby, my mind flooded with strange visions of what the experiment could entail. I remembered studying the long-term effects of child abuse, as they translated into adulthood, for the last exam. Surely, that wouldn't be a potential topic for the experiment.

I didn't want anyone delving into that part of my psyche. Ever.

As I got tangled up in my daydreams, the

remaining students were called away for their own experiments. Before too long, I was the last one left. Again. An uneasy feeling flowed through my system, because the déjà vu felt all too expected, all too planned.

Sighing aloud, I carried my satchel over my shoulder and rose from my chair in the lobby. I trudged across the carpet with my head down, desperate to go back to my apartment and sleep. Nightmares of my past had tormented me the night before, but I didn't want to revisit them now.

"Miss O'Connell," a cheery voice called. I looked up to find Cabel with a pen and clipboard in his hand. "Ready?" He turned on his heel as I followed, letting him guide me down the hallway.

"For what exactly?" I searched for the nearest elevator, intent on heading home and curling into a ball on the couch. But when Cabel grabbed my elbow, I gave him a second glance.

"Your experiment," he answered, furrowing his brow in frustration. "It's today."

"I know it's today," I snapped back, already irritated. "My experimenter didn't show up." I brushed past him and continued down the corridor, desperate to find a place to rest my head.

"I'm your experimenter." The strength of his voice followed me, traveling down the hall.

I slowed my feet and turned back around, not believing a word he had said. "What?" Cabel stepped towards me, his icy blue eyes dilating at the pupil. I thought that was odd, considering the bright fluorescent lights overhead. "Come with me," he pressed, his steady gaze authoritative and haunting, "unless you want to fail."

I forced myself to swallow, then followed Cabel down several long, winding corridors, until he finally led me into an empty room and shut the door behind us. Cabel flipped the light switch on, to reveal a small rectangular table with two wooden chairs on either side of it. I glanced around the room, spotting a couch against the left wall and a sink by the lone window at the back of the room. The blinds were drawn.

I flinched when Cabel shut the door, and then jerked one of the chairs out from the table. "Have a seat," he ordered. Obedient, I tossed my satchel onto the couch and took a deep breath.

"Yes, Mr. Jones." I sat down with my feet flat on the ground, my hands gripping the seat.

"When are you going to stop calling me that?" Cabel stood in front of me, hovering.

"When are you going to stop calling me Miss O'Connell?" I countered.

The edge of Cabel's mouth lifted into a smirk, though he didn't allow the smile to linger. I held his gaze, looking up at him through my eyelashes, playful and coy. Cabel narrowed his eyes at me in return, but not out of malice. He was thinking, wondering, considering.

"Roll up your sleeve," Cabel instructed, staring at my black long-sleeved t-shirt.

"What?" I stared up at him in confusion, while

Cabel merely sighed. All at once, he leaned forward, grabbed my left wrist with one hand, and pushed my shirtsleeve back with the other, until the fabric became a bunched mess around my elbow. I held my breath at the touch of his skin against mine, while Cabel rocked back on his heels and placed his hands on his hips.

"Put your arm on the table," he said, alarming me further. I rested my left arm on the table beside me and turned my palm up towards the ceiling. When Cabel collected a black box from the TV stand and placed it on the table, I began to sweat.

"Don't I have to sign a disclaimer first?" I piped up, questioning his order and method of experimentation.

"We'll get to that," Cabel confirmed.

Just as he unlocked the box and opened the lid, our eyes met with frantic delight. I forced myself to swallow, my gaze shifting from Cabel to the table. What was inside of the box?

Suddenly, an alarm sounded overhead, sending a violent ringing through my ears. Cabel shut the box and returned it to the TV stand, then jerked me out of the chair. Before I could react, an announcement came over the PA system.

"Attention all students, faculty, and staff. Please evacuate campus immediately. This is not a drill. Find the nearest exit and leave now. All classes are cancelled until further notice."

The announcement played on a continuous loop, while the alarm rang on and on.

"Cabel, what's going on?" I tried to swallow, but there was no more than a hard, relentless lump in my throat. Distracted, Cabel released me and moved to the door, deftly clicking the lock in place. "Cabel?" He grabbed the chair I had been sitting in and pushed it in front of the door, then snatched the table and remaining chair off the floor and did the same.

Cabel weaved his fingers through his hair, those blonde locks becoming disheveled and unruly. His head snapped back when someone began pounding their fist against the door. I looked into Cabel's eyes and noticed that his soft blue irises had thinned around two deep circles of black.

Without any warning, Cabel grabbed my arm and steered me towards the window. He drew the blinds back, and then pushed the window open to reveal our only way out.

"No!" I protested, struggling against him. Cabel grabbed my shoulders and shoved me towards the window. I stomped his foot with my shoe and kicked him in the knee, but Cabel wrapped his arm around my waist and leaned his head on my shoulder.

"Climb down the railing and go next door," he whispered. "Take the stairs to the third floor and wait for me in the second room on the left. It's the janitor's closet." I felt his warm breath in my ear, his words more comforting than the vice-like grip he had around me.

"What?" I whimpered, tugging at his arm. "But, I don't understand."

"Trust me," he pleaded in earnest.

The banging against the door only grew louder, as I tried to rationalize, tried to think, tried to decide what to do. I didn't know if I could even trust Cabel. I hardly knew him. But in that moment, I realized how badly I wanted to.

"Is this part of the experiment?" I craned my neck around to look back at him, my eyes dancing across the planes of his strong, chiseled face.

"No," he mouthed, his lips so close to mine that they nearly touched. For the briefest moment, Cabel looked at peace with the world, gazing into my fearful brown eyes. But then the door burst open, and Cabel picked me up and tossed me out the window.

Chapter 5

Bracing myself, I stuck my hands forward to weaken the impact of the fall. But when I landed on the concrete, my right ankle twisted with just enough pressure to bring tears to my eyes. I cried out in pain, clutching my ankle between my hands.

"Run!" Cabel shouted. I looked up from the flat of my back to find him leaning through the window, his hands on the railing. "Run!" he repeated, waving me towards the closest building.

Hesitant at first, I placed my palms on the cool cement, and then eased myself onto my left foot. Just as I regained my balance, a gunshot sounded overhead and Cabel's body lurched forward.

"Go," he groaned, just before they pulled him away and closed the window.

Panic-stricken, I hobbled my way to the nearest building and took the elevator to the third floor. When the doors opened, I spotted a group of men across the hall, leaving the stairwell. They all looked the same: tall, strong, armed, dressed in black shirts, shoes, pants, and masks. With my injured ankle, I didn't stand a chance.

Terrified, I stayed on the elevator and rode it to the fifth floor. When the doors opened to an empty landing, I got off in search of a place to hide. I traveled with ease, as I twisted the knob to every door, only to find that each one was locked, and I had no key to get in.

The elevator dinged, sending a slow, lingering heat through my body. On pure adrenaline, I rushed into the stairwell and watched through the window in the door, as one of the armed men stepped off. The elevator doors shut behind him, and he moved with stealth, searching the fifth floor.

Sinking to the ground, I kept my back to the stairwell door. Questions raced through my mind, as I succumbed to the fear, letting it lance through me like a knife. Where was Cabel? What had they done to him? Where were they taking him? And if they truly had taken him, then what were they going to do to me?

I listened to the elevator chime again, and then opened my eyes. When the silence remained, I mustered enough courage to lean on my left foot and look through the glass.

The man was gone.

Breathing a sigh of relief, I slowly hobbled down a flight of steps to the fourth floor. As I approached the stairwell door and looked in the window, the man appeared through the glass. Horrified, I let out the most piercing scream, and then raced up the steps on one foot. While I struggled to keep my balance, the man pushed the door open and came after me.

He grabbed my leg and dragged me down the staircase, showing no remorse when my chin slammed into one of the steps. I cried aloud, then twisted onto my back to find him standing over me with his gun aimed at my face.

Helpless, I gazed into his cold, dark eyes with every fiber of my being and willed him not to hurt me. "Please," I begged, covered in a sheen of fear and sweat. "Let me go." My lower lip trembled, as a sticky substance trickled down my chin.

I tasted the sweat.

I tasted the salt.

I tasted the blood.

"Please," I wailed, crying on the floor. "Let me go."

The man cocked his head to the side, peering down at me through his black mask. I shuddered at the sight of his chilling, callous glare, as he searched every inch of my face, weighing me, judging me, deciding whether or not I deserved to live. Then, just as calmly, he straightened his neck and uttered, "No."

Cabel burst through the stairwell door and bashed the man in the head with a fire extinguisher. The man's knees buckled and he collapsed, seemingly unconscious. I lay at the bottom of the stairs, sobbing with relief, while Cabel set the extinguisher on the ground and searched the man. When his icy blue eyes met mine, I gazed up at him in silent gratitude.

He knelt down before me and took my face in his hands. I hung my head and sobbed aloud, letting my emotions overwhelm me, as the tears multiplied. Never losing focus, he removed his tie and wrapped it around my ankle, forming a makeshift bandage. I placed my arm on his shoulder until he was finished, thankful for his gentle touch.

Quietly brooding, Cabel tucked my hair behind my ear, and then grabbed the man's gun. I watched through blurry tears, as he stood up and tucked the gun into the waistband of his pants. "We have to go," he said, gingerly taking my arm. I nodded, though kept my eyes down, while he led me to the elevator.

When we heard footsteps approaching from down the hall, Cabel picked me up, pulled me into the janitor's closet, and shut the door behind us. I squealed in pain as my right foot came down on the floor, but Cabel clamped his hand over my mouth to quiet the noise.

"Calm down," he breathed. "Are you trying to get us killed?"

As my eyes adjusted to the darkness, I was able to make out the faintest image of a mop in the corner. Except for the sliver of light beneath the door, Cabel and I were in complete blackness. I couldn't even see his face. Upset, I grabbed his wrist and peeled his hand from my mouth.

"I don't understand what's going on," I

complained. "Why won't you tell me?"

The doorknob began twisting in a wild manner, as I let out a fearful gasp of air. Cabel wrapped his arm around my stomach and pulled me to the back of the closet with him, then covered my mouth with his hand again. I tensed up when Cabel's left forearm glided over my smooth stomach, forcing the hem of my shirt up to my waist. His hand felt strange and foreign over my bare skin, though I kept my eyes straight ahead.

When the doorknob stopped rattling, I listened to the sound of my heavy breathing, as loud air blew out of my nostrils. Cabel relaxed his grip, though only slightly, to keep me wrapped in his embrace. I could feel his heart beating in quick, pounding rhythms, while my back lay flush against his chest.

Cabel rested his chin on my shoulder, as the slightest bit of stubble from his beard tickled my skin. His hot breath blew across my neck and past my ear, sending tingles down my spine. Before I could react to the sensation, a strange object rolled through the gap beneath the door and filled the room with smoke.

Chapter 6

The poisonous vapor burned my throat, clouding the entire room with thick, toxic fog. I could hardly see my own hand, much less Cabel, as the smoke continued to rise and widen. Violently coughing, I grabbed the collar of my shirt and pulled the fabric over my mouth, to prevent the gas from reaching my lungs.

"Cabel!" I yelled, reaching out for him with my other hand. "Cabel!" My eyes stung and my nostrils felt like they were on fire, but he was all I could think about. "Where are you?"

I felt Cabel's grip around my arm, as he pulled me to the ground. But the air was so thick with smoke, that I couldn't do more than wiggle within his grasp. "Come on!" he shouted, nudging me towards a patch of clear air in the floor. Confused, I eyed the smokeless hole warily, unable to understand what I was looking at.

"What?" I coughed back at Cabel, putting both hands on the floor, while my knees dug into the hard ground. Growing impatient, Cabel grabbed my hips and dropped me into the hole.

I tumbled downward, landing on a wooden

staircase with a noticeable thud. Wincing at the pain in my ankle, I slid my way down the steps and into an old, abandoned basement. Alone in the dark room, I crawled onto the floor and sat up with my back against the wall. I was definitely going to have bruises tomorrow.

Cabel fell through the trap door more gracefully, and then clambered down the steps in haste. "Are you all right?" He unfastened the top button of his white dress shirt and crouched down before me. I kept my eyes on the ground, unable to form words. My shoulders ached, as I lolled my head back against the wall, dreadfully fatigued.

"Yeah," I exhaled, tired of the pain. Anxious, I looked down at my ankle and noticed how quickly my foot had begun to swell. Cabel's black tie had come loose, and now that I had fallen down the stairs, the throbbing had only gotten worse.

Cabel refastened the tie, hurriedly wrapping the material around my ankle. I winced, though only slightly, when he knotted the tie at the heel of my foot. "I'm sorry," Cabel whispered. His hand lingered near my ankle, while his cool blue eyes scanned my face.

"At least we can breathe now," I murmured, offering the faintest of smiles.

Dust floated down from the ceiling above, as we both looked up at the sound of banging. Whoever was standing outside the janitor's closet had yet to find a way in. Determined, Cabel rose to his feet and walked towards one of the countless windows lining the far left wall.

"What are you doing?" I groaned, too concentrated on the pain to think of anything else.

"I'm getting out of here." Cabel found a stack of bricks in the corner, near the window, and picked one of them up. "Are you coming or not?" he asked.

I hesitated, eyeing him quietly from across the room. "My ankle," I explained. "I can't walk on it." I shrugged my shoulders, as if there was nothing else that either of us could do.

"So, I'll-"

"Just go and get help," I interrupted. "I'll stay here."

Beyond exhaustion, I took a deep breath and closed my eyes, not wanting to fight anymore. When I opened them, Cabel was standing over me with a look of fury on his face. I had never seen him so still.

"What?" I looked up at him, lethargic and weary. Cabel shook his head, and then placed his hands beneath my armpits, jerking me up like I was a little girl. "Ah," I sucked in a deep breath of air and scowled.

"Come on," he demanded. "I'll carry you." Cabel bent down and tucked his arm beneath my knees, while his other arm supported my back.

"Stop!" I protested, nearly losing my balance. "I don't want to be carried."

Cabel withdrew from my body, gaping at me in shock.

"Go!" I commanded. "You're wasting time!"

Cabel glared down at me, his husky blue eyes sending tingles down my spine. When he released me, I felt a twinge of disappointment, though I couldn't understand why. Cabel crossed the room, grabbed one of the bricks, and tossed it through the window. Glass shattered across the floor, as Cabel looked back at me for the last time.

I heard his feet hit the ground, after he climbed through the window and landed outside. The banging upstairs grew louder, as I lifted my face to the ceiling. Dust rained down from up above, choking and blinding me. Distressed, I turned my head back to the broken window, but Cabel was gone.

Realizing my mistake, I crawled across the floor and hobbled onto my left foot. Just as the sound of footsteps came barreling down the hidden staircase, I gritted my teeth and hurled my body through the window. The grassy ground was harder than I had anticipated, but I was thankful for the row of bushes that concealed my presence.

A car door slammed as I ducked behind the bushes, in an attempt to remain unseen. Footsteps sounded nearby, beating across the street pavement. I peeked through the bushes and spotted a silver Toyota parked in the road, whose engine had been left running. The driver's side door was hanging open with the keys still in the ignition. When I looked back over my shoulder, Cabel was climbing through the window again.

"Cabel!" I whispered, knowing that the men must have broken into the basement by now. "Cabel!" I quietly yelled, terror lancing through me, as he stepped inside.

No matter how much my ankle hurt, I couldn't watch Cabel blindly lead himself into the lion's den. Scared for his life, I pushed the pain out of my mind and moved close enough for him to hear me. "Cabel!"

He turned around and stalked towards the window, his face etched with concern. He had been looking for me in the empty room. "There you are," he said.

"Cabel, we have to get out of here!" I leaned against the window sill, planting my left foot in the grass.

Suddenly, the ceiling began to collapse, and one of the armed men tumbled down the staircase and into the basement. I gasped aloud, reaching for Cabel's hand through the window. But I couldn't grab him before the man on the floor fired his gun.

Chapter 7

NOOO!" I wailed, watching in slow motion, as the bullet pierced through the top of Cabel's left arm. Reaching through the window, I grabbed Cabel by the collar and jerked him towards me. He climbed over the ledge and dropped down in front of the bushes, never minding his injury. Instead, he ran towards the running car with his hand around mine, mercilessly dragging my body behind him.

When we reached the car, Cabel pushed me inside and helped me crawl over the console, until I slid down into the passenger's seat. Then he jumped into the driver's seat beside me and closed the door. I could still hear gun shots as we sped away, barely escaping the view of the two armed men who had just climbed out the window. Struggling to catch my breath, I glanced over at Cabel. He had yet to crack beneath the pressure.

"Cabel," I sternly declared. "What's going on?" He eyed the rearview mirror and kept his hands on the steering wheel, ignoring me. "Cabel!" I slapped his good arm, and he flinched.

"Ow!" he growled, narrowing his eyes at me,

before his focus returned to the road. "What was that for?"

"Tell me what's going on," I demanded. "Why are there men chasing us? Why did the whole campus have to evacuate? Cabel, what's happening?"

"Finally," he chuckled, heightening my aggravation.

"What?" I snapped back.

"It's about time you started calling me that."

I rolled my eyes and exhaled, staring through the front windshield. When I glanced back at Cabel, he was smirking. But then I noticed blood dripping onto the car seat from his arm.

"Cabel, you're hurt," I sympathized. "We need to go to the hospital."

"I'll be fine," he replied, brushing the matter off. I scowled, because I couldn't fathom why he wouldn't be concerned about the fact that a bullet was in his arm. Somehow, I resisted the urge to scold him and tried a more subtle approach.

"How bad is it?" I studied the handsome, rugged bone structure of his face and swallowed. I desperately wanted to reach out to Cabel, but was afraid that I might hurt him.

"Just a flesh wound," he managed, forcing a smile. "I'll be all right."

I watched Cabel as he drove, studying the blood stains on his shirtsleeve. Tears welled up in my eyes, though I held them at bay. Never before in my entire life had I wanted to go home so badly.

"How's your ankle?" he asked.

"It's swelling," I reported. "Cabel, I'd like to see a doctor."

"You can't go to the doctor," he rebuffed. "Not now."

"Why?"

"Because you just can't. All right? I'm sorry, but no."

And so began the argument that lasted into the night. We drove for hours and hours, crossing state lines and breaking speed limits, until I relinquished my anxiety and dozed off. When a car door slammed, I stirred awake to find Cabel trekking into the forest.

"Cabel!" I loudly whispered, calling after him, though he didn't hear me. On edge, I sat up in my seat and looked through the car window. We were pulled over on the shoulder of a dark two-lane road that was surrounded by acres of woods on either side. The land stretched on for miles, with no sign of street lamps, buildings, or civilization.

We were in the middle of nowhere.

I looked on with intrigue, as Cabel walked in front of the headlights and batted away several clustered branches at the entrance to the forest. Thinking he had lost his mind, I furrowed my brow and sank into the passenger's seat. But then, Cabel lifted one last branch and revealed an old, rusty gate that had been hiding behind the trees.

After pushing the gate open, Cabel scurried

back to the car and climbed inside. He shut the door behind him, and then drove straight ahead, shivering from the cold. "It's freezing out there," he said. I quickly glanced over at him, before flicking my eyes back to the pathway before us.

Like steady clockwork, Cabel drove through the gate, parked the car, then hopped out to shut the gate and conceal it behind the branches once more. When Cabel returned to my side, he shifted the car into drive and put his foot on the accelerator, as we plunged deeper and deeper into the cold, dreary forest. I looked through the windshield, scanning the ongoing stretch of woods and all that those dark, twisted thickets entailed. Anyone could have been lurking out there, watching us.

"Cabel, I don't like this," I confessed. "I don't know where we are. I wouldn't know how to get out of here if I needed to."

"It's okay," he assured me, though the forest appeared more frightening by the minute. "You'll be with me." I felt Cabel's eyes on me, but couldn't turn my head away from the glass.

After what seemed like an eternity, we arrived at an old, run-down cabin that looked like the closest thing to shelter around these parts. "We have to get rid of the car," Cabel muttered, catching me off guard, as he pulled the keys from the ignition.

"What?" I turned to face him, panicking. "Why?"

Cabel popped the trunk and removed the few belongings he had, tossing them at the front door of the cabin. Then, he climbed back inside the car and drove until we reached the edge of a wide cliff. "Come on," he urged, failing to answer my questions. "I can't move it alone."

"Cabel, I-"

"Just help me push her off, and then we can go inside," Cabel begged, though it felt more like a command.

"Her?" I criticized.

"Jealous?" he fired back.

I rolled my eyes and exhaled, refusing to say anything more on the subject.

When Cabel walked around the car and opened my door, I heard a hoot owl making his nightly calls from the treetops up above. Widening my eyes, I lifted my head to watch the creature from a distance, and then turned to Cabel. At least we weren't alone out here.

Cabel let me lean into him, as he helped me out of the car. It was the only way to keep the pressure off my ankle. Once I caught a glimpse of the blood stains on Cabel's white dress shirt, I tried not to complain. But I couldn't help whimpering, when I had to stand on both feet to help Cabel with the car.

"Ready?" Cabel looked over at me, now that the car was in neutral, and there was no time left for dawdling. I placed my right foot on the rear bumper of the car, to relieve the pain in my ankle for the moment, and then nodded.

Cabel squatted down and positioned his hands on the tailgate, while I tried my best to do the same. "All right," he prompted, bracing himself. "One-two-three."

As Cabel and I pushed, the car moved forward, soon picking up speed. I attempted to lift my foot from where it had been resting on the bumper, but my shoe wouldn't budge. When I looked down, I realized that my shoelace had come undone and was currently hanging on to the frame of the car with all its might. In an instant, the car began coasting along without our help, and I fell to the flat of my back.

"Cabel!" I screamed, while the car dragged my body towards the edge of the cliff.

Immediately reacting, Cabel grabbed both of my hands and jerked me backwards. I gasped at the sudden movement, feeling like my bones might snap. "Take your shoe off!" he yelled.

I couldn't use my arms, because Cabel wouldn't let go of them. So, I nudged the toe of my left shoe along the heel of my right shoe. But then the car jolted forward, and Cabel fell down, as the car started to drag him behind me.

Without any warning, Cabel lunged for the rear bumper and batted my shoe away, crushing my foot in the process. I cried out in pain and collapsed on top of Cabel, while heavy, exhausting tears streamed down my face. He helped me sit up, and then we both watched, as the car went over the edge of the cliff, eventually crashing to the ground.

I buried my face in my hands and wept, overcome by the throbbing discomfort in my foot. Intuitively, I knew that I had broken it. Cabel stood up and approached the edge, looking down at the forgotten car below. I hoped that getting rid of it had truly been the best idea, because now we really were stranded in the middle of nowhere.

Utterly drained, I dried my eyes and looked up to find Cabel looming before me. He reached out and wrapped his hands around my waist, intending to help me to my feet. But I didn't want to move. Not yet. Perhaps I could sit out here all night and shiver, maybe even freeze to death. Surely, it would be better than whatever else the future had in store.

"No," I protested, pushing him away.

Cabel exhaled, as I watched his breath materialize in the space before me. "We need to go inside," he announced.

I rested my chin on my left knee and said, "I don't want to."

"Finley," he scolded. "We need to go inside. You need to go inside."

"I don't need to do anything right now with you!" I lashed out, glaring up at his ever-widening eyes. Enraged, Cabel leaned down and picked me up without the slightest difficulty. "Put me down!" I demanded, beating my fists against his chest like an unruly child.

Cabel ignored every word I said, as he carried me back to the cabin in his arms.

Chapter 8

Cabel walked into the cabin and shut the door behind us, gingerly laying me down on a soft mattress. I closed my eyes and shivered, angry with Cabel, angry with myself, angry with life. When I opened my eyes again, Cabel was rummaging through a closet in the corner. I looked around the room, making out what I could in the darkness.

There was a small window on the far right wall, with a thin, ragged curtain hanging over it. Streaks of moonlight poured through the holes in the fabric, casting shadows onto the mattress. Reluctant, I turned my head to the other side of the room, noticed another wooden door by the closet, and vaguely wondered how long we would have to stay here.

Cabel struck a match, and then lit a column-shaped candle, setting it down on the small bedside table next to me. I re-examined the room in its newfound light and spotted a few cobwebs hanging from the walls and ceiling. Following my gaze, Cabel batted the cobwebs away with an old dishrag, and then looked over the place himself.

"Well," he sighed, "there's a bathroom in

there." Cabel pointed to the door by the closet. "And I think we've got some food in here." I watched him sort through cans of vegetables and meat on one of the shelves in the closet. "I can get us fresh water from the river," Cabel added, before turning away from the closet. He walked over to the window and pulled the curtain tight over the glass, though just as much light came through the holes.

Exhaling, I lay back on the mattress and relaxed. What more could I do, other than accept the fact that we were stuck in the wilderness? For now, only the owl knew where to find us.

"How does it feel?" Cabel stood at the end of the bed and grabbed my foot less tenderly than he could have.

"Ow!" I griped. "What was that for?" Cabel unraveled his black tie from my ankle, and then applied a great deal of pressure to my foot until I flinched.

"We're going to have to re-break a few places in your foot," Cabel said, as if he were reporting the weather. I cocked my head to the side, hoping that I had misunderstood.

"What?" I sat up in the bed and jerked my foot away from him.

"We need to do it now," he pressed, "before it starts to heal."

I widened my eyes in terror, as Cabel moved towards the closet, where he retrieved bandages, two gauze rolls, and a bottle of Jack Daniels

Tennessee Whiskey. When he came back to the bed, I pulled my knees into my chest and swallowed.

"Come on," Cabel said, insistent as ever. He grabbed my foot and began running his ice cold hands over the bruised tendons.

"Cabel," I inhaled, "haven't I been through enough today?" His frosty blue eyes scanned my face, as he withdrew his hands from my foot.

"Fine," he declared. "Let it grow back wrong, but don't come crying to me."

"Cabel," I called, as he turned his back to walk away. "I'm sorry."

Blowing hot air through his nostrils, Cabel sat down on the edge of the bed and gazed at me. I straightened my posture and stared, not used to having a man in my personal space. He lifted his hand to cup the side of my face, and then ran his thumb along the edge of my mouth.

I stopped breathing.

"How's that lip?" he asked.

"I don't know," I managed to say.

My eyes traveled to Cabel's mouth, as I found myself admiring his full, lush lips, so much like a sweet forbidden apple that I wanted to sink my teeth into. The thought disarmed me entirely, but I resented myself for thinking it.

"Here," Cabel said, handing me the bottle of whiskey.

"I don't drink," I asserted.

"Finley," he groaned. I couldn't understand

him. Maybe he really was rotten after all.

Like most men.

Like all men.

Shouldn't I know?

"I'm *not* drinking that," I snapped back.

"It's for the pain," he explained. "Your foot, I know it hurts."

"I don't need it."

Cabel eyed me wearily, weighing my words. "All right," he succumbed.

But Cabel didn't know that I could handle the pain, that I was raised on pain, that I'd felt the buckle of the belt more times than the leather.

"Let's clean your face first," Cabel suggested. My shoulders sagged in relief, though I was only delaying the inevitable. "Here," he said, offering the Jack to me again. "To clean your lip. It's all we have." I glanced down at the bottle, and then back up to Cabel.

"No." I shook my head, testing his patience further. "You do it."

"Are you sure?" Cabel looked into my eyes, his dark, nearly black in the dim light.

"Yes." I nodded.

Cabel soaked a piece of cloth with whiskey, eyeing me carefully from beneath his lashes. I held my breath, when he moved closer and grasped my chin in his hand. As he pressed the damp cloth to my lips, I sat perfectly still, practically turning to stone. Cabel could be gentle.

"It doesn't look like you'll need stiches," he

assessed, relatively cheerful.

The cut in my bottom lip stung like fire, but I didn't move a muscle. Instead, I looked into Cabel's eyes, watching him, as he cleaned the dried blood from my chin and jawline. When he finished, I pinched the skin around my wrist, preparing my body for the real pain.

"You can do it," I declared.

Cabel furrowed his brow and blinked several times, as if he didn't understand what I had said. "What?" he whispered, gazing at me in awe.

"My foot," I clarified. "Do it." Cabel studied me carefully. "Break it."

Wasting no time, Cabel rose to his feet and walked to the foot of the bed. I felt my whole body tense up, but I knew that if I didn't let him break it now, I would have to pay for it later. So, I took a deep breath and stretched my legs out on the mattress.

Cabel handled my foot with delicate care, though his hands were still cold, as he felt for the broken places. The tears were already beginning to well up again, that hard lump re-growing in my throat. Before I could cry, Cabel rested my foot on the bed and let go.

"What's wrong?" I wondered, ready for the pain to be over.

"We don't have to do this," he assured, offering me an escape. "Not if you really don't want to." Cabel lowered his lashes, patient and respectful. He was letting me decide.

"It's okay." I smiled at him in the dark. "I trust you."

And I did, though maybe I shouldn't have. I barely knew anything about him. But I reasoned that if he was going to hurt me, he would have already done it by now.

Cabel smiled back, and it made me wonder how many times he had heard those words.

I trust you.

Bracing himself, Cabel took my foot in his chilly hands and gazed down at me. "Tell me if it hurts too much and I'll stop, okay?" I nodded, averting my eyes. I spotted a pillow beside me and placed it over my face. "All right, ready?"

"Yeah," I yelled through the pillow, though I wasn't.

"Okay," he hesitated, stalling. "So, I'm going to go ahead and-"

Aggravated, I peeked my head out from under the pillow. "Would you just be a man, and do it already?" I flexed my arms as I repositioned the pillow over my face.

Cabel grabbed my foot, and this time, I knew he meant it. I tensed up all of my muscles right before, reacting to Cabel's frigid touch. If not for the fear, I probably would have been shivering from the cold.

In an instant, I heard the crack, and then felt the pop. To handle the pain, I sucked part of the pillow into my mouth and bit down as I screamed. Tears streamed down my face, though I felt lightheaded. In time, I let go, slowly releasing my grip on the pillow.

Chapter 9

When I woke up, the candle beside the bed had burned out, but my eyes quickly adjusted to the darkness. I pulled the bed sheet back and found my right foot wrapped in bandages. The throbbing was still there, but the pain seemed to be bearable enough for now.

I heard Cabel in the bathroom and turned my head to look. He had left the door cracked open just enough for me to see his reflection in the mirror. My cheeks blushed crimson red at the sight of his shirtless figure in the glass. Cabel poured whiskey onto his arm, cursing aloud as he did so, and then slammed the bottle down on the counter. I watched him wrap a thick layer of gauze around the middle part of his bicep, covering the bullet hole. Warmth flooded through me, because I realized that our troubles were just beginning. Cabel had been shot, and I couldn't walk. What was next?

"Can't sleep?" Cabel walked over to the bed and lit the candle on the table beside me. I shook my head. "Is it your foot?" he asked. "Does it hurt? Is that why you can't sleep?"

"No," I murmured, glancing up at the ceiling. When I felt his eyes on me, I turned my focus back to him. "Where's your shirt?" I wondered. Cabel smirked down at me, even though I was being entirely serious. "What?" Cabel pointed towards my torso, where I found his shirt draped over me, on top of the bed sheet. "Oh," I said, understanding his playful demeanor.

"I didn't want you to get cold," he admitted. I felt my cheeks redden further at that.

"Thank you," I replied, looking away, so he couldn't see how nervous he had made me.

Cabel headed towards the closet, where he grabbed a glass bottle full of clear liquid.

"Here," he said, handing it to me.

"What is it?" I sat up in the bed and took the tall bottle in my hands.

"It's water," he answered, "from the river." Leery, I unscrewed the cap and lowered my nose to the rim. Cabel chuckled, placing his hands in his pockets, as he watched me. "I thought you trusted me," he said.

The liquid smelled harmless, so I took a small sip, careful not to press the glass to the tender cut on my lower lip. As the cool water slid down my throat, I realized how thirsty I was and began taking huge gulps, until I started to choke.

"Slow down," Cabel kindly ordered. He patted my back, and then took the bottle away from me.

"I want more," I declared, wiping the moisture from my mouth with the back of my hand.

Cabel gave in to me and handed the bottle back. I drained half the container, so relieved to have fresh water. It felt like the closest thing to home since we had left campus.

"Aren't you cold?" I returned the bottle to him, concerned. He set the water down by the candle, and then shoved his hands back in his pockets. I noticed goose bumps rising on his arms, though he would be the last to admit to them.

"How does your foot feel?" he asked, casually changing the subject.

"It's okay," I replied, watching as he paced the floor in front of the bed. "How did you know what to do?" I wondered. "How did you know how to break it?"

"I've had my fair share of broken bones, Miss O'Connell," he boasted. I tried to ignore the fact that he hadn't said Finley.

"How?"

"My older brother," he revealed. "Growing up, we didn't exactly see eye to eye."

"He hit you?" I stilled my eyes on his face, hoping he couldn't see through me.

"Attacked is more like it," he corrected, "but yes, he hit me. More times than not."

"Did you tell anyone?" I lowered my eyes to the bed, then glanced back up at Cabel. "Your parents?"

He scoffed at my remark, exhaling loudly. "They would have called me a coward."

"The police?"

"You think I should have reported my family to the police?"

"I did." I let the words sink in for a moment, feeling Cabel's blue-eyed stare. In a moment of weakness, I had said too much. And this was why I had built the wall — to keep from letting anyone in.

"What?" Cabel blinked three times, and then crossed his arms, thinking he had heard me wrong.

"I hate to be the one to tell you this, Cabel. But sometimes, blood is the last thing that is thicker than water."

"What?" Cabel took a step back, confused.

I relaxed into the mattress, and then pulled my knees into my chest. Even though I'd brought up my past, I didn't want to talk about it now. I didn't want to talk about it ever.

"Cabel, I'm cold," I complained, shivering in the bed. My teeth were already starting to chatter, and the sheet on the mattress wasn't getting any thicker.

"What do you think I am?" he barked. "I gave you my shirt. Do you want my pants now too?"

Resting my head on the pillow, I opened my big, brown eyes and gazed up at him in innocence. I'd never shared a bed with anyone before, especially a grown man. But now, I realized that I had to.

"Lie down with me," I begged, my eyes watering in an instant. Cabel froze in place, as his lips formed a hard, resilient line. "Please," I whispered.

"I don't know, Finley."

"What is it?" I leaned up on my elbow and scanned his face with concern.

"It's just," he hesitated, ruffling his fingers through his blonde locks. "I don't know if I can do that."

"Why not?" I snipped, aggravated.

"I just can't." He shrugged his shoulders, as if there was nothing he could do about it. I pursed my lips together and scowled, because he wasn't acting like a man at all.

"You'd rather us both freeze to death than touch me. Is that it?"

"No," he denied, already starting to shiver. "Not at all."

"Then what is it?" I searched his husky blue eyes in the darkness. "Do you not understand the concept of body heat? Or, did they not teach you that at Cornell?" Cabel looked into my eyes without blinking, unfazed by my insulting remark. I couldn't understand why.

"I'm a professor," he began, solemn and earnest. "And you are my student."

"So?" I furrowed my brow at him in disgust.

"So that's one line that I'm not willing to cross," he declared, firm in his conviction.

Frustrated, I rolled over, turned my back to him, and then pulled his shirt up to my neck for warmth. The fabric smelled like him, and I liked that smell.

"Here!" I yelled, tossing the shirt over the bed at him. "I don't need your stupid shirt anyway."

Cabel sat down on the floor with his back pressed against the wall, facing the side of the bed. I watched him slip his arms through the shirtsleeves, and then fasten every button until he reached the collar. Angry, I blew out the candle and rolled back onto my side, facing the window.

"I'll bet you didn't have any brothers," Cabel spoke. "Did you?"

My ears perked up in curiosity, though I was still mad at him. "No," I muttered. "Why?"

"No sisters either?" he asked.

"No," I repeated. "How did you know that?"

"You're not used to being told no," he claimed. "Only child syndrome?"

I sat up in the bed and looked over my shoulder at him. "I may have been an only child, but that doesn't make me a brat. I've been told no plenty of times, not that you would understand what that feels like," I bitterly remarked.

"What is that supposed to mean?"

"You're the golden boy, Cabel. Perfect face. Perfect job. Perfect life. I'll bet you've heard yes more times than I can count. So don't you dare act like I always get what I want. I've never had anything that wasn't earned." My chest rose and fell, as I struggled to catch my breath. I hadn't intended to give a speech, but that was what had happened.

"You're wrong," Cabel responded. "I never

said you were a brat, and I'm not perfect." He tilted his head to the side and confessed, "I'm far from it."

Chapter 10

Sunlight poured in the next morning, shining through the curtain holes over the window. I blinked several times, struggling to open my eyes in the blinding brightness of the day. Cabel stood at the edge of the bed and leaned against the wall. He was eating an apple. Shirtless.

"How did you sleep?" he asked between bites.

I refused to answer and glared at him instead. As I sat up in the bed, I found Cabel's white dress shirt spread out over my torso and wondered when he had put it there.

"Why do you have such a problem with keeping your shirt on?" I held out the shirt in my hand, as Cabel waltzed over with a smug expression on his face.

"I'm happy to see that you're a morning person," he quipped, taking the shirt from me. "Hungry?" Cabel extended his hand to show me his red, half-eaten apple. "Want some?"

I glanced at the fruit, and then back to Cabel. What was he doing? Teasing me? After the way he had behaved last night, I couldn't help feeling upset.

"I'd rather starve," I said through a pair of gritted teeth.

The light drifted from Cabel's eyes, as the smirk on his face disappeared. He finished the apple and tossed the core into an empty trash can. I didn't want to ask where the fruit had come from, because then he would know how badly I wanted it.

Determined to make my own way, I slid out from the bed sheet and dropped my left foot to the floor. "Here, let me help you," Cabel offered, rushing to my side. He grabbed my shoulder and prepared to lift me off the bed.

"Stop!" I griped. "Let go of me."

Cabel stepped back, offended. "I'm just trying to help you, Finley."

"After last night, I don't think I want any help from you," I snarled, hating the venomous words that poured from my mouth. Cabel let his shoulders sag, his arms falling limply at his sides. I got out of the bed and hobbled my way over to the door with Cabel at my heels.

"Finley," he called after me. "Please, let me help you."

I lifted my hand to the doorknob and sighed. "I'll be back later," I said. "Don't follow me, and please, while I'm gone, put your shirt back on." With a reluctant twist of the handle, I opened the door, and then scampered off into the woods.

I must have hobbled around the wilderness for hours, because time moved like slow molasses. My foot ached, but I pressed onward, eventually coming across a beautiful river past the trees. I limped down to the bank of the river, kneeled onto the ground, and cupped my hands in the water. Despite its frigid temperature, I was extremely thirsty, so I drank as much as I could hold, until white flakes began to fall from the sky and float along the surface of the river.

"It's snowing," I realized, pleasantly surprised. "It's snowing!"

Excited, I lifted my hand in the air and watched snowflakes collect on my palm. By the time I climbed back up the bank, the snow started coming down faster and harder. But I was too distracted to recognize that I was caught in the middle of a snowstorm.

Instead, I made snow angels in the thick layer of white powder that covered the ground. When the flurry picked up, I headed back to the cabin, terribly cold and hungry. Why had I ever left? Why didn't I take that apple?

Soon, I found myself lost in the winter wonderland nightmare that I had received. But I had asked for it, because of the simple fact that I wouldn't let Cabel take care of me.

I struggled to find my way back in the bitter cold, eventually resting at the base of a pine tree. My crippled foot was screaming for warmth and comfort, but the opposite was all I could give. I was inadvertently helpless.

The bleak winds turned violent, sending down

patches of blinding snow. Everything I had seen in the dark was now unrecognizable in the light.

"Cabel!" I yelled, though I knew he couldn't hear me. "Cabel!" I could hardly spot the sound of my own voice in the storm. How would he be able to?

I rested my head over a network of tree roots and dug my fingers into the frozen earth. As I lay there, defeated and shivering, I felt a gathering of soft, smooth plants brush against my palm. Curious, I sat up and shoveled the snow away with my hands to reveal a crowded mass of tall, dirty white mushrooms.

I gazed down at the lonely, plentiful stalks with ravenous delight. Looking around the woods, I checked my surroundings in the snowy blizzard. Cabel was nowhere to be found, and I had no way of knowing how to get to him. So, I pulled every mushroom from the ground and stuffed my face, until the snow had covered the spots where they had been.

At first, the mushrooms left me feeling sated, blissful, and relieved. But then a strange sensation flooded through me, and all of the snow on the ground began to disappear. In time, the sky cleared, sending me into a state of intrigue and wonder. I stood up and tried to find my way back to the cabin, but was too distracted by all of the blooming flowers to keep walking.

The sun turned orange, though its circumference became slightly tinged with pink. I smiled up at the pretty colors, and they smiled back, granting me the use of my injured foot. Giggling, I danced my way through the glorious wilderness, full of sweet floral fragrances and all of the enchanting, abundant nature that spring holds.

During my journey, I found myself moving towards a pleasantly robust fruit tree, whose limbs were hanging heavy with the weight of apples. My eyes widened with innocent curiosity, as I waltzed over to the towering tree. When I stopped beneath the leafy green branches, I giggled, because the tree was calling my name, begging me, enticing me to draw near.

"It's all right," the tree coaxed. "You can come closer."

Just as I stretched my hand out to grab a shiny red apple, a familiar voice stopped me.

"Finley," Cabel called. He ran towards me, grabbed my shoulders, and looked me in the eye. "Are you insane?"

"What?" I snickered.

"In the middle of this storm, are you trying to get yourself killed?" Cabel planted his hands on my face, forcing me to look up at him with a pair of wide eyes.

"It's so pretty," I gushed. "Look at the flowers, the trees... so beautiful."

"What's wrong with you?" Cabel asked, shaking my body.

I laughed, nearly toppling over. Cabel steadied my balance, and then opened my palms. He found specks of mushroom in my hands and furrowed his brow, panicking.

"Finley, what did you do?"

I looked up at him in confusion, blinded by the sun. Turning around, I glanced back at the heavenly fruit tree that had been sent here just for us. "Is that where you got your apple?" Cabel searched my face, then narrowed his eyes at the apple tree. "I want one," I chirped, leaning into his chest. "My apple," I slurred, liking the strange way my words formed.

Frightened, Cabel squatted down on the ground, as his fingers danced across the forest floor. When Cabel found more mushrooms, he froze. My face lit up with elation, while I stood there beaming.

"Finley, did you eat these?" He quickly rose to his feet, though the motion was blurred. Cabel looked like a carton, all wavy and distorted.

"Yeah," I laughed.

"How many did you eat?" Cabel towered over me, crimson anger surrounding his aura.

"You're a pretty color," I noted, watching his eyes dazzle and blink, as they turned purple.

Cabel squeezed my arm and cornered me, getting in my face. "How many, Finley?"

I stared down at the ground, and then looked into Cabel's kaleidoscopic eyes. They shifted in the same way a chameleon changes color.

"All of them," I answered. "More?" I pointed to Cabel's mushroom-filled hands and grinned.

But Cabel threw them on the ground and jerked me away from the fruit tree. In that moment, I stumbled to my knees and collapsed, feeling sick to my stomach. Nausea overwhelmed me, and I didn't want to move.

Cabel picked me up and carried me through the wilderness, as the pain in my stomach grew worse. "Put me down," I pleaded. "Please." When Cabel released me, I sank to the ground, leaned forward on my palms, and vomited more than I ever had in my entire life.

I felt Cabel behind me, holding my hair back, as my body continued to purge the toxins I had ingested. Embarrassed and uncomfortable, I sat up and leaned back against Cabel. "Just leave me," I said. "I don't want you to see me like this."

My hands were shaking, the frightening heat coursing through my blood. With all of my weight on Cabel, I could feel his heartbeat against my back. He leaned his head on my shoulder and whispered, "I'm not leaving you."

"I wish you would," was all I managed to get out, before I vomited five more times.

Feeling lightheaded and weak, I lolled back, unable to hold myself upright. Cabel wrapped his arm around my stomach and pulled me into his lap. I began to see the snow again, as my hallucination slowly dissipated.

"It's the mushrooms," I drawled. "They're poisonous."

"I know."

"I'm sorry, Cabel." I turned my head back to look at him, as he held me in his arms. "I didn't mean to."

"I know you didn't," he sympathized. I felt myself drifting away, off to some other place. I couldn't keep my eyes open any longer. "No!" Cabel shouted, shaking my arms. "Stay with me."

"I was just so hungry."

Chapter 11

I felt a cool hand against my forehead, as my eyelids fluttered opened. The room was filled with candlelight and Cabel was sitting on the bed. I had never been more thirsty.

"You're still burning up," Cabel commented. Beads of sweat ran down my face, my chest, my back. When the moisture ran into my eyes, the stinging sensation filled me with unease.

"Water," I groveled, stroking my fingers against my throat. I closed my eyes until Cabel returned with a tall glass bottle of fresh water.

Cabel held the back of my neck, as he tilted my head forward and placed the bottle against my lips. I gulped the water, letting the cold, refreshing liquid run down my throat.

"More?" Cabel prompted.

"Yes," I rasped. "Please."

Cabel returned the rim to my mouth, and I sucked every last drop down like a nursing infant. When he refilled the bottle, I drank more, but the layer of sticky sweat continued to cover my body.

Silent, Cabel placed a cold cloth over my forehead, and then wiped the sweat away from my cheeks, throat, and chest. My temperature wasn't decreasing any time soon, and we both knew there was hardly any fight left in me.

"Cabel," I mumbled, hardly an audible breath. "I'm sorry, I-"

"Don't start making your apologies to me now," he growled, though not out of anger.

"I'm so hot," I complained, unable to keep my eyes open.

"I know you are." Cabel brushed my dark hair out of the way, and then pressed the cold cloth against my skin again.

"You should have left me," I spoke, only opening my mouth enough to breathe.

"I would never leave you."

Lethargic, I forced my eyes open, though only slightly, and gazed up at Cabel. In the dim lighting, his blonde tresses looked darker. But those frosty blue eyes remained the same, as enchanting as a mystical ice castle, from some fairy tale I had read as a child. I didn't believe in Prince Charming, but Cabel sure looked like him.

Cabel placed his hand against the side of my face, his skin the temperature of ice. In any other scenario, I would have shied away, but his arctic fingers felt like heaven. Pleased, I leaned my cheek into the palm of his hand and sighed. "Why are you so cold?" I asked. Cabel chuckled, and it was then that I noticed he was shivering.

"We're in the middle of a blizzard, Finley," he said.

I turned my head ever so slightly and looked out the window. Violent winds continued to blow through the trees outside, even though day had turned to night.

"Isn't that ironic?" I noted.

"What?" he wondered, his deep voice soft and subtle.

"I'm too hot. You're too cold." Cabel widened his eyes, and then rose to his feet. I looked on in confusion, as he began unbuttoning his shirt. "Please. No," I said. "Not with the shirt again. I don't need it. Trust me." Unfazed, Cabel peeled his shirt off, stepped out of his shoes, and then began unbuckling his belt. "Cabel, if you're in the mood for strip poker, I can assure you that this is not the time or place," I affirmed, slowly mumbling each word.

"Look," Cabel demanded, as he stepped out of his black dress pants. "You said it yourself. You're too hot. I'm too cold."

"You didn't like the idea of sharing body heat yesterday," I countered.

"We were both freezing yesterday, Finley," Cabel declared.

"And now?" I gazed at him, intrigued.

"And now you're the Sahara Desert, and I'm Antarctica," he insisted through a pair of chattering teeth.

Seeing that Cabel was right, I held his gaze and nodded. "Okay."

Immediately, Cabel walked around to the

other side of the bed, pulled the sheet back, and sank into the mattress. Before he could lay a finger on me, I turned my face towards him and groaned.

"What's wrong?" Cabel asked.

"The sheet," I explained. "Get it off me." I tried to kick the sheet away with my good foot, but didn't possess the energy. "It's too..." I moaned, drifting, "hot."

Cabel pushed the sheet away, then pressed the back of his hand against my forehead. I felt him tug at my shirtsleeve, but didn't protest. "You need to get out of these clothes, Finley. You'll never cool down if you don't."

I looked down at my black long-sleeved shirt and thick blue jeans. The fabric was sticking to my skin in an uncomfortable manner, because both pieces of clothing were drenched with sweat, my sweat. "I can't," I whimpered, feeling helpless. I wasn't sure if I even had the strength to lift my arms. "You do it," I begged.

Hesitant at first, Cabel lifted the hem of my shirt, as his hands felt like ice on my skin. I lay still, not caring that he was going to see my matching bra and panties, merely because I was that unwell.

When Cabel dragged the shirt over my head and tossed it onto the floor, I felt less heated already. Then, Cabel unfastened the top button of my blue jeans, slid the zipper down, and stuck his fingers into the waistband of my jeans. As his frigid fingertips brushed over my legs, I found myself admiring Cabel's strong, lean physique, until he finally freed me of those hot, binding pants and chucked them on the floor near my shirt.

Wearing nothing more than a pair of boxer shorts, Cabel lay down on the bed and pulled me into his embrace. I gasped at the feel of his icy cold arms and legs, as he wrapped them around me. But when my body acclimated to his frigid touch, I began to relax.

Cabel held my body tightly to his own, his fingertips digging into the bare skin of my back. Relieved by his close embrace, I rested my warm cheek against his cool chest, as Cabel sighed in contentment. He was the oasis to my Sahara Desert.

When the fever finally broke, my temperature began to regulate, and I found myself needing warmth from Cabel, just as much as he needed it from me. He pulled the sheet over the two of us, and then slid his arm back under the cover and around my waist. I felt Cabel's warm breath on my shoulder, his lips nearly touching my collar bone, while the blizzard outside eased into a quiet night.

We lay together in the darkness without a need for words of comfort or assurance. I had no idea what had happened, where we were, or who we were hiding from. But as Cabel breathed steadily beside me, I closed my eyes and let go. The candle burned out, as I fell asleep in his arms.

Chapter 12

My foot woke me in the morning, throbbing and cursing from within. I winced at the pain, longing for relief from the discomfort. Cabel slept soundly beside me, a gentle snore escaping his parted lips. When I couldn't stand to lie still any longer, I peeled Cabel's arm from my stomach and let my legs dangle over the edge of the bed. As I planted my left foot on the floor, my arm reached for the bedside table to steady my balance. But the previous day had left me feeling so drained, that I stumbled into the table and fell to the ground.

"Ah," I inhaled, sucking in a deep breath. I pulled my injured foot towards me and tried to sit up.

"Finley?" Cabel woke up and spotted my disgruntled state on the floor. He jumped out of the bed and pulled his pants on, then bolted towards me. "What happened?"

"What do you think?" I gritted my teeth, not wanting to cry. "I fell."

Cabel leaned down and gingerly picked me up off the ground. I put my arms around his neck, as he lowered me onto the bed. Aching, I grabbed his right arm at the bicep and tearfully gazed into his eyes.

"I want to see a doctor," I cried. "Please. Take me to a doctor."

Cabel hesitated, then swallowed, as if he were forcing a small knife down his throat.

"I can't," he said. "I'm sorry."

Tears flooded my cheeks, while Cabel became a blurry image before my eyes. Rolling over, I buried my face in Cabel's pillow and wept like I hadn't in years. I couldn't handle the fear anymore. The fear of not knowing. The fear of knowing too much. The fear of not knowing enough.

"Why are we here, Cabel?" I sobbed, turning back to face him. "Why am I here?"

Cabel blinked, looking away.

"Why did you bring me here?"

"To protect you," he answered.

"To protect me from what?" I yelled back at him, though the force of my emotion only worsened the pain in my foot.

Cabel pressed his lips together, unresolved and angry.

Good, I thought to myself. *I hope you're as angry as you've made me.*

"Tell me!" I demanded.

"I can't!" he shouted, glaring down at me. "They already think you know more than you do, and I," he stopped himself, then cast his eyes to the ground. "I already know too much."

"Who Cabel?" My pulse was racing, but I couldn't quit now. "Who are you talking about?"

"You don't need to know."

"And why not?"

"Because it's not important."

"Yes it is!" I snapped back.

"Finley, just listen to me." Cabel hovered before the bed, waving his hands in the air as he spoke. "You don't need to know anything right now," he said. "It's for your own good." When I shot him a look of fear and helplessness, Cabel came closer. "Don't you trust me?" He sat down on the bed and cupped my cheek in his hand.

"In the beginning, yes." I averted my eyes, and then glanced back at Cabel. "But now? I don't know."

"Finley, please," Cabel begged, brushing his thumb beneath my eye, along my cheekbone.

"Give me a reason to trust you, Cabel," I muttered. "And I will."

His hand fell from the side of my face, as he stared at the floor in anguished defeat. When he stood up and made for the door, I felt a new sense of panic overwhelm me. Surely, he wouldn't leave me here stranded.

"Where are you going?" I wondered.

"Just outside, to get snow for your foot." Cabel shut the door behind him as he left. I lay back in the bed and cried.

* * *

When the sun set, I felt the throbbing sensation in my foot return. Cabel went out to get more snow, and when he came back, it had been nearly ten hours since we had spoken.

I ate a can of sliced carrots and potatoes, though the slimy vegetables were hardly appetizing. Cabel treated my foot with tender care as I ate, icing my injury down with a new clump of snow. If he wasn't going to take me to a doctor, then he would need to act like one until my foot healed.

"Does it feel any better?" Cabel waited for an answer, to which I gave no reply. In fact, I didn't even raise my head from the can of vegetables, too preoccupied with my meal. "Finley, I'm sorry, okay?" I dipped my spoon down low, gouging a thin potato slice at the bottom of the can. "Please, stop it with the silent treatment. I can't take it."

I placed the spoon in my mouth and swallowed the vegetable whole, fixing my eyes on the food that remained in the can. Beyond his limit, Cabel snatched the spoon out of my mouth and jerked the can away from me.

"Hey!" I yelled, infuriated. "Give that back!" Cabel paced the floor beside the bed and began eating what was left of the carrots and potatoes. "Cabel!"

When he ignored me, I leapt from the bed and tackled him to the ground. He dropped the spoon and can, as they both clattered to the floor beside us. Paralyzed, he glanced up at me from the flat of his back, stunned that I had knocked the wind out of him.

With Cabel searching for breath beneath me, I sat down on the floor beside him, hardly believing what I had just done. Before I could arrange my thoughts, Cabel grabbed me and began tickling my sides.

"Ah!" I screamed out in laughter. "Stop it!" I shouted. "Cabel, stop!"

But he continued to punish me, showing no mercy, as I squealed aloud. I wrestled with Cabel fiercely, trying with all my might to break free from his grasp. Eventually, Cabel turned the tables on me, and I lay on the flat of my back beneath him.

In that moment, Cabel stopped tickling me, as my laughter turned to a shy smile. Cabel's expression mirrored my own, until his face became serious, pensive, contemplative. I felt my cheeks blush scarlet red, when he brushed his fingers along the edge of my jawline. Cabel's pupils dilated, and he lowered his face above mine. But then, suddenly, something in Cabel's demeanor changed, though I couldn't understand why. I sagged my shoulders in unexpected disappointment, as he sat back on his knees and helped me to my feet.

Later that night, Cabel and I huddled together for warmth, neither willing to discuss what had happened between us earlier on the floor. Instead, I lay my head on the pillow, with Cabel's arm protectively draped over my stomach. Despite the strange tension between us, I was glad to have Cabel near.

"Finley, you asleep?" Cabel whispered in the darkness.

"Yes," I hissed back. He chuckled, and the sound carried across the room.

"Do you remember what you said before? About reporting your family to the police?" My whole body tensed up. I didn't want to talk about this. "Well, did you?"

"I'm an orphan," I admitted. "I don't have a family."

"Oh," he replied, shocked. "Finley, I'm sorry. I shouldn't have asked."

Cabel settled into the mattress, soon drifting off into a calm, peaceful sleep. I felt the rough stubble of his unshaven face, as he placed his chin on my shoulder. Sinking into the warmth of his embrace, I tried to shield myself from the nightmares. But they had no intention of staying away.

Chapter 13

The next morning was better in some ways and worse in others. The pain in my foot had momentarily subsided, but I had barely slept a wink during the night. Memories that I had rather forget were brimming on the surface of my mind, and I didn't know if I would be able to keep them at bay for much longer.

When I opened my eyes, the space next to mine was empty. I stretched my hand out and felt the mattress. The place where Cabel had slept was still warm. Out of the corner of my eye, I spotted Cabel buttoning up his white dress shirt, as he headed towards the door.

"Where are you going?" I whined, combing my fingers through my hair.

Cabel turned around and looked at me, as though he had been caught trying to escape while I was still sleeping. Worried, I sat up on my elbows and watched him linger near the doorway. Cabel was hiding something.

"There's something that I have to go take care of," he said, vague as ever.

"Well, let me go with you." I pulled the bed

sheet back and swung my legs over the edge.

"No," Cabel demanded. "Stay here. I won't be gone long."

Narrowing my eyes at him, I pressed my palms into the mattress and exhaled. "Cabel," I scolded, "I can hardly walk. Why would you leave me here by myself?"

"I'll be right back," Cabel insisted. "I promise." He turned around and reached for the doorknob.

"I may not be here when you get back," I murmured, staring down at the floor. Cabel froze for a second, then watched me slip into my long-sleeved t-shirt and blue jeans.

"What are you doing?" he growled.

I pulled my socks over my feet, and then began to put my left shoe on. "If you're not staying here, then neither am I."

"Finley," he crooned, gazing at me from across the room. When I offered no reaction, Cabel sat down beside me on the bed and tugged at my chin. "Please, don't go. You don't know what's out there."

"And what is?" I looked him squarely in the eye, neither of us breaking contact.

"Finley, you're just going to have to-"

"Trust you?" I interrupted. Cabel's hand fell from my face, but his eyes remained on mine.

"You don't understand," he reasoned, raking his fingers through his blonde hair.

"I wonder why," I countered, infuriated. "You haven't told me a single thing since we've been here. How could I understand?"

I finished tying my shoelace, and then placed all of my weight on my left foot, in an attempt to stand. But Cabel grabbed my arm and pulled me back down on the bed beside him. Seething, I glared into his eyes, unable to withdraw from his strong grip.

"Cabel," I protested, "let go of me."

When he released my arm, I sighed in relief, and then held onto the bedside table, as I stood up from the mattress.

"This isn't how I wanted to say goodbye," Cabel muttered.

Leaning on the edge of the table, I turned around to face him. "Well then how did you want to say goodbye?" I gave Cabel my full attention and waited for him to answer my question. But he merely scanned the length of my face, his own etched with worry and frustration. I couldn't bear to look at him anymore.

Disappointed, I leaned back on my good foot and averted my eyes. If Cabel couldn't be honest with me and completely divulge all that he had kept secret, then I wasn't interested in listening to him say another word.

"Just go, Cabel," I softly spoke.

He kneaded his palms together, withholding thoughts, feelings, everything, like always. His eyes stayed on the floor for a long time, as if he knew the moment was fading fast, and he wanted to do everything in his power to prolong it. Eventually, he rose from the bed and turned towards me.

"I never meant to hurt you," he confessed. "Please, believe me when I say that I never meant for any of this to happen."

I crossed my arms over my chest in defiance. Cabel stood before me, staring, pleading, begging for forgiveness with his cool, gentle blue eyes. But I didn't want to forgive, because I didn't want to forget.

"All right, I believe you." I gazed into Cabel's eyes, showing him that I meant what I said. But Cabel remained unmoved. "Are you leaving now?" I snapped, rolling my eyes. There was no need to lengthen the pain.

"No," Cabel breathed, his eyes on my mouth.

Without a second thought, he stepped close enough to bridge the gap between us, took my face in his hands, and pressed his lips to mine. I shut my eyes, absorbing the wonderful sense of euphoria, as Cabel pushed me up against the wall. Impatient, he forced my lips apart with his mouth, deliberate, yet tender. I felt his fingertips at the border of my jawline and throat, as he tilted my head forward, bringing his face closer to mine.

Fighting for air, I took a gasp of oxygen before Cabel clamped his mouth to mine once more, molding our lips together in a way that made me forget how to speak, how to think, how to breathe. To keep from fainting, I placed my hands on his shoulders and maintained what balance I had left. When Cabel pulled away, I opened my eyes and struggled to catch my breath. Feeling his hands on my face, I gazed up at Cabel, as he leaned my head back. I couldn't have avoided his warm, sultry stare if I had tried.

"I would have given you the whole world, if you had just asked for it," he whispered, looking over me with unguarded longing and affection.

Swallowing, I furrowed my brow and glanced up at him in concern. Before I could respond, Cabel claimed my mouth again, as his hands traced patterns down my neck. Lost in the moment, he tugged at my lower lip, still sore from the recent cut, but I felt no pain. A hushed whimper escaped my parted lips, a sound more vulnerable, more raw, more real, than I had ever expressed before.

In an instant, the wall of protection and solitude that I had built up over the years came crashing down. Cabel had busted through the bricks and aimed straight for my heart. I tried to resist the overwhelming rush of emotion that his physical touch had unleashed within me, but Cabel was like a force of nature, unpredictably constant. In that precious, private moment, I knew that I would fall in love with Cabel Jones, because I already had.

Cabel planted a surprisingly sweet kiss at the corner of my mouth, and then pulled my wrists from his shoulders. When I opened my eyes, he dropped my hands, looked at me for the last time, and turned away. I stood with my back against the wall, paralyzed, as he walked out the door, slowly shutting it behind him.

"Cabel," I called, still in shock. I approached the door and twisted the handle, discovering that he had locked me inside. "CABEL!" I yelled, knowing he couldn't hear me. "Cabel! Let me out of here! PLEASE!"

Growing restless, I hobbled over to the window and quickly discovered that it wouldn't budge. Frustrated, I snatched the worn-out curtain from its frame and flattened my hand against the wall, to keep from losing my balance. The fabric made a decent wrap over my elbow, which I used to smash the glass, until I had broken a large enough hole in the window to fit through. I crawled out of the broken window and landed on my good foot.

Outside, the snow from last night's blizzard had begun to melt. The temperature remained chilly, but as the sun burst forth, breaking through the clouds, I felt a surge of warmth in my cheeks. Filled with light, I raised my head to the sky and smiled.

That was when I heard the first gun shot.

Chapter 14

The second came faster, sharper. And by the third, my heart was beating so fast that I could hear pulsing in my ears.

Taking off, I hobbled through the wilderness on my left foot, placing the smallest amount of pressure on my right. In no time, it became clear to me that I was lost, trapped, possessed by the forest and all of her tantalizing trickery.

The trees seemed taller, towering over me like some legion of soldiers designed to keep me imprisoned. I thought I might search for the river, to have a sense of direction in these woods, but as I trekked deeper, the sound of running water appeared to be an impossibility. As my feet grew tired, I sat down at the base of a tall pine tree to rest. But then I heard the sound of someone moaning, and my entire body froze.

Turning my head, I looked over my shoulder and followed the noise with my eyes. At that moment, I realized exactly where I was in the wilderness. Just past the stretch of pine trees, I spotted the edge of a cliff, the same cliff that we had pushed the car over just days ago. The scenery looked different in the light, but I knew that was the place.

I stood up and made my way towards the cliff, then got down on my knees and peered over the edge, in search of the car. Instead, I found Cabel, sprawled out on a ledge down below, crying out in pain. Terrified, I climbed down to the shelf of rock that extended outward from the cliff, ignoring the discomfort in my foot.

When I reached the ledge, my lungs painfully compressed, as all of the air escaped them. Cabel lay still before me, his white dress shirt covered in crimson. I unbuttoned the shirt and exposed Cabel's lean, muscular torso, that was now pooling over with blood. Cabel had been shot three times, just as I had heard. My hands moved over his body, counting the bullet holes.

Two in the stomach.

One in the chest.

Cabel was going to die.

"No!" I cried, holding his face in my hands. "Cabel, I'm sorry," I whimpered. "I'm so sorry."

I lay down beside him and wept, wrapping my arm protectively over his stomach, as he had done for me. The tears fell in heavy streams, pouring down my cheeks like rainfall. The act of crying felt abusive, like my insides had become a sponge that someone was constantly squeezing dry.

In time, his body grew cold, and the color began to leave his skin. I wrestled with the realization that there was nothing I could do for him. But I didn't want to let go. I didn't want to admit that my golden boy was fading away.

I placed my head on Cabel's chest and listened to his slowing heartbeat. His breathing grew weak and shallow, until he murmured aloud. "Brother," he wheezed, his ice blue eyes settled on the clouds above.

"What?" I whispered. "What did you say?"

I leaned back on my knees and swept my thumb across Cabel's cheekbone. He coughed, pure red blood staining his teeth, as his body turned still. In a moment I would never forget, he drew his last breath, and then blankly stared at the bright blue sky overhead.

"NO!" I wailed, pressing my head against his neck.

I didn't believe it.

I couldn't believe it.

Cabel wasn't dead.

I grabbed his arms and wrapped them around me, as we lay together on the ledge. A pool of tears collected in the space between his neck and shoulder, but I tasted more blood than salt. I stayed with him for hours, talking, crying, whispering, until my arms and legs became numb from lack of movement. Even as the sun went down, I refused to leave Cabel's side.

For hours, I replayed through memories in my mind. Our few nights in the cabin. The experiment that never happened. My moment of humiliation at the grocery store. That first day we met in the rain, when Cabel exchanged his book with mine. All too soon, I realized that I had forgotten to tell Cabel that I loved him. Heartbroken, I studied his face in the moonlight, coming to terms with the fact that his soul now rested elsewhere.

My ears perked up at the sound of rustling leaves, as voices carried down from the cliff above. Without any warning, harsh light shone into my eyes, temporarily blinding me. I held my arm against my head to shield my eyes and noticed a man with a flashlight.

"There she is," he declared, quickly climbing down to us. The man grabbed my arm and tried to peel me away from Cabel, but I wouldn't let him.

"NO!" I exclaimed, fighting and scratching, clawing my way back to Cabel.

But the man was too strong, as he tossed me over his shoulder and climbed back up to the edge of the cliff. My injured, shoeless foot scraped against the rock, forcing me to cry out. I sobbed at the pain in my foot, though it hurt less than the sweltering ache in my heart.

When the man reached the top, he set me down on the ground, and then rose to his feet. In the moonlight, I could see his gray hair and stocky build. From the looks of his complexion, I guessed that he was in his mid-fifties and hadn't exercised any time in recent years. He placed his hands on his knees and leaned over, catching his breath.

"We've been looking for you," he rasped, standing up straight.

Lifeless, I peeked over the edge of the cliff, knowing that Cabel was still down there. When the man touched my hand and took a knee before me, I glanced at him through a pair of tear-filled eyes.

"I can't leave him," I whimpered. "Please don't make me."

"Everything is going to be all right," he said. "Come with me."

Nodding, I hobbled to my feet and let him guide me over to a parked car. When he opened the back door and helped me inside, I thought that I might start crying again. The man noticed and stuck out his hand. "Monty," he greeted, pleasantly polite.

I took his hand and let him shake mine. "Finley," I replied.

"I think we're going to get along just fine." Monty withdrew his hand, and then shut the door.

I gasped aloud, flinching at the sight of a young man in the passenger's seat.

"Sorry," he murmured. "I didn't mean to scare you." He turned back in his seat and smiled. I felt all of the blood drain from my face, as I widened my eyes in disbelief.

He looked just like Cabel.

Part II
The Lonely Girl

Chapter 15

Monty climbed into the driver's seat and shut the car door behind him. He turned around and looked at me, but my eyes were on the ghost of Cabel. Even though I blinked several times, the blonde, blue-eyed golden boy remained.

"So," Monty began, turning back to the steering wheel. "Cabel never told you he had a twin?" I knitted my brows together, feeling the start of a sudden migraine.

"No," I responded, careful in how I revealed my ignorance. "He didn't."

"They're identical, you know," Monty conveyed, starting the car.

"I can see that," I darkly declared. Monty eyed me in the rearview mirror, and then drove through the moonlit forest.

Looking out the window, I felt myself losing what connection I had developed with Cabel in the cabin. Tears surfaced at the border of my eyelids, but I didn't want them. Instead, I sank into the back of the car and closed my eyes.

Within minutes, Monty opened my door and took my hand in his, leading me out of the car and into the plain, brown house before us. I leaned into Monty's shoulder and glanced up at the tall, unfamiliar structure. Two men emerged from the front door, dressed in matching black suits. They walked to the car and pulled Cabel's twin out of the front seat.

For the first time, I noticed that his hands were handcuffed behind his back. He caught me looking over my shoulder at him and smiled. The way his lips curved upward sent a chill down my spine, because his playful smirk looked just like Cabel's.

Monty helped me over the threshold, and then motioned towards a sofa in the left hand corner of the room. I took a seat, glad to have a moment to rest my foot in a building with central heat and air conditioning. Scanning my surroundings, I observed a modest kitchenette at the back of the room with a fridge and bar. A flat screen TV hung on the wall facing me, while the rest of the room was decorated with the occasional chair, end table, or lamp. My mind felt cloudy, as I peeled my dirty sock off to examine my throbbing foot. It was swelling again.

"I'll have our doctor take care of that for you," Monty offered.

"Thanks," I replied, searching for understanding in his eyes.

The men brought Cabel's twin into the room, and then steered him towards a wooden door by the TV. "Take him to the back of the house,"

Monty ordered.

"What did he do?" I questioned, forgetting my place. Warmth filled my cheeks, as four pairs of eyes found mine. Cabel's twin glanced over my body with a look of familiarity, searching, discovering, remembering.

Monty turned his head back to the men and opened the door. "Go on," he pressed. They silently nodded, then stepped through the doorway and into a long, narrow corridor. From my spot on the couch, I could see multiple doors on either side of the hallway. I couldn't help wondering which one they were taking him to and what would happen to him when they did.

"Would you like something to eat? You must be starving." Monty shut the door, and then stepped towards me.

"Okay," I breathed, feeling dizzy.

Monty strolled over to the kitchenette and reached for a plate in the overhead cabinet. "How long have you known Cabel?" he inquired, while I turned my eyes to the door that the rest of the men were now on the other side of.

"Not long," I answered, cautiously eyeing Monty, as he placed a pot of soup on the stove.

"Cabel was a good man, Finley," he admitted. "One of the best I've ever known."

I crossed my arms over my chest and exhaled, flicking my eyes to the floor. For a solid five minutes, I felt certain that I was going to throw up. But when Monty came over to the couch with a bowl of soup and a sandwich, I forced myself to smile.

"Thank you," I said, as Monty set the plate in my lap. Famished, I looked down at the stacked sandwich, complete with lettuce, tomato, turkey, cheese, and mustard. A handful of potato chips lay scattered around the sandwich, but I could only stare.

Monty put the bowl of soup on the end table beside the couch, and then handed me a silver spoon. "I'll get you some water," he announced. When he returned with a glass, I gazed up at him in admiration and took it.

"Who are you?" I probed, biting my tongue after it was too late. "I'm sorry," I backpedaled, "I shouldn't have-"

"No," Monty interrupted, holding his hand up. "It's all right." He dragged a chair in front of me and sat down in it. "I'm a friend, Finley. Just an old friend."

Trusting him, I nodded, and then proceeded to eat my meal in silence. When I was done, Monty cleared the dishes away, forgetting what I had said earlier. "Would you like to take a shower before the doctor arrives? She's on her way over right now."

Casting my eyes downward, I looked over my clothes and realized how dirty I was. "Okay," I agreed.

Monty helped me to my feet, and then took me through the door and down the corridor. As he opened a closet and retrieved a fresh change of clothes for me, I felt my blood run cold all over. Down the hall, I could hear the sounds of a man being beaten.

"What are they doing to him in there?" I asked, pointing my finger towards the end of the hall.

Monty let out a sigh, and then handed the fresh set of clothes to me. "Nothing that he doesn't deserve, I'm sure." I watched Monty's brown eyes stare at the last door on the left.

"What's his name?" I wondered. "Cabel's twin, I mean. What is his name?"

"Seth," Monty responded. He opened one of the doors on the right, revealing the bathroom to me. "Towels are in the cabinet, and there's a box of soap on the shelf."

Nodding, I stepped inside the bathroom and shut the door behind me, thankful that there was a lock. I stripped my clothes off and stepped inside the shower, then ran the water until it was scalding. The hot mist spattered out of the showerhead, taking my breath away, as I stepped back on my good foot.

When I noticed that dirty red liquid was circling the drain, I sat down in the tub and cried. Cabel's blood was all that I had left of him, and now it was gone, washed away with the dirt and sweat that had built up on the surface of my skin. I pulled my knees into my chest and rocked back and forth beneath the shower, until the hot water turned cold.

"Finley?" I heard a knock at the door, recognizing Monty's voice on the other side. "Are you all right in there?"

"Yes!" I yelled. "I'll be out in a minute." Grabbing a fresh bar of soap, I lathered and scrubbed until every layer of grunge had melted away. I thought about Seth and the terrible noises coming from the end of the hall. What could he have possibly done to deserve that?

Drained, I shut the water off, stepped out of the shower, and grabbed a towel. The mirror was covered with condensation from the steam, so I swiped my palm over the glass and studied my reflection with scrutiny. My big, brown eyes looked bloodshot and empty, like I hadn't slept in days. Pushing my dark, wet hair over my shoulders, I exposed the pale, freckled nature of my skin. The apples of my cheeks burned bright red, as a result of the hot water, no doubt, and the cut in my lip looked much worse than it felt. But my face, as a whole, appeared dull and emotionless, lacking color, lacking luster, lacking life.

After drying off, I slipped into the clothing that Monty had given me: a pair of tight black jeans and a simple gray sweater. My own clothes lay in a pile on the floor, so I scooped them up and carried them out the door with me. Monty was waiting in the hall and took the pile from me without asking permission first. "I'll just throw these in the washing machine for you," he declared.

"Thanks," I said, even though I didn't appreciate his hands on my things.

I looked down the hallway and listened for the unpleasant moaning that I had heard earlier, but there was nothing more than silence.

"The doctor's here," Monty informed. "Would you like to see her now?"

"Yes." I glanced back over my shoulder at the last door on the left, and then followed Monty out of the corridor.

An attractive woman with red, shoulder-length hair sat on the sofa where I had eaten earlier. Monty shut the door behind us, and then gestured towards the woman with his hand.

"This is Dr. Rose, and she'll be taking care of you today." Monty stayed by my side, as I took a seat in the chair opposite her.

"Finley," I said, extending my hand for her to take.

Dr. Rose smiled. "It's nice to meet you, Finley," she chirped, her green eyes bright and shining. After shaking my hand, her tone turned serious, and her gaze shifted to my foot. "So tell me what happened."

With Monty in the room, I glossed over the truth and told her that I had fallen down the stairs. Dr. Rose listened attentively, nodding every so often to show me that she understood. After being alone with no one but men in the house, it was nice to talk to someone who knew what it meant to be a woman.

Dr. Rose wrapped my foot in a makeshift cast, then told me to keep it elevated as much as possible, to keep the swelling down. She stressed that I stay off my foot and visit another doctor, who could provide an x-ray, crutches, and a real cast, when I returned home. After Dr. Rose left, I found myself wondering why she hadn't found it odd that I was out here in the middle of the wilderness with all of these men. Monty must have paid her a great deal of money to keep quiet.

"I'll be right back," Monty piped up all of a sudden. He walked out the front door and closed it behind him. When I heard the sound of another man's voice outside, my body stilled, and I perked my ears up to listen.

"Where's Seth?"

"In the back," Monty curtly answered.

"And the girl?"

"She's here. Rose has already been by."

"Good," the man said. My mind drifted through memories past, as I tried to figure out why his voice sounded so familiar. "Well," he continued, "let's talk to her then. There's nothing else we can do at this point."

Twisting my fingers together, I stared at the front door in fear, imagining who could be on the other side. When the doorknob began to slowly twist, I felt sweat collecting at the back of my neck. Before I was ready, the door opened and Monty stepped through. In that moment, I recognized the man with him the way you recognize the face of an old friend who you just can't seem to put a name to.

He crossed the threshold and let Monty close the door, then stepped towards me with a smooth, graceful stride. I held my breath, immediately spotting the strange hue of his eyes: light brown with a ring of deep green around the pupils. His hair looked the same, mostly black, with streaks of gray at his temples.

"Hello, Finley," he greeted. "It's nice to meet you." I widened my eyes in astonishment, feeling strangely starstruck.

He didn't have to tell me his name, because I already knew who he was.

Chapter 16

I'm Blain Ulrich," he said with a smile.

"I know who you are," I brusquely countered. "I've seen you on TV."

Ulrich's smile broadened into an ever-widening grin, which brought the dimples on either side of his cheeks to life. Already into his late forties, Blain Ulrich was a Harvard man, former judge, loyal husband and father, who was currently in the process of claiming a home at the White House. An excellent debater, Ulrich had caused quite a stir in recent months, for being unapologetically harsh, and, quite frankly, too honest where his views on the country were concerned.

But I didn't care about Ulrich's politics or the fact that he was running for President at a time when the polls were in his favor. I just wanted him to flash his usual, complacent smirk and send me on my merry way. I just wanted to go home.

"Well, I'm sure you have," Ulrich declared, self-satisfied narcissist that he was. He waltzed over to the bar and poured himself a glass of hard liquor, Scotch whiskey to be exact. I hated him already. "I see you've met my running mate."

Ulrich glanced at Monty, then splashed an infinitesimal amount of water into his drink.

"Oh," I squeaked, feigning interest. "You've chosen running mates already? I didn't know. I'm not interested in politics."

Ulrich chuckled, a deep, dark sort of laughter that made the hair on the back of my neck stand up. "No honey," he patronized, "I haven't won the nomination yet. But when I do, Monty will be my man."

"You sound awfully sure of yourself," I noted. Ulrich stepped towards me with his glass in hand, the ice clinking around as he moved.

"How old are you, Finley?" Ulrich placed his free hand at the back of my chair, and then leaned over me, his face too close to mine. I could smell his breath.

"Nineteen," I coolly replied.

"Nineteen," Ulrich echoed, sipping at his Scotch right in front of me. He stared into my eyes as he drained the glass, failing to miss a drop.

"Yeah."

"Well," he paused, taking a step back. "I guess you're wondering what you're doing here, Miss Finley."

"Yes," I hissed, narrowing my eyes at him in irritation. "It would be nice to have some sort of explanation."

Ulrich walked past me and slumped onto the sofa, then set his empty glass down on the end table beside him. I caught Monty out of the corner of my eye, lingering near the doorway. Despite the fact that both men were strangers to me, I felt more comfortable knowing that Monty was nearby.

"I'm guessing you're acquainted with Seth?" Ulrich asked, his eyes settling on mine a little too comfortably.

"Yeah," I acknowledged. "He's Cabel's twin brother."

Ulrich hunched his shoulders forward, letting his elbows slide down to his knees, as he folded his hands together. "Seth is part of a terrorist organization," Ulrich relayed, holding my gaze. "A powerful terrorist organization that is searching for political secrets. My political secrets." Before I could ask Ulrich what that had to do with Cabel, he explained further. "Political secrets that only a handful of people know about. Cabel was one of those people."

Flicking my eyes to the floor, I let the words reverberate in the room. Why did Ulrich have to talk about Cabel in the past tense? Why must **is** so quickly become **was**?

"Why would Cabel know about your political secrets?" I furrowed my brow, then glanced at Ulrich, awaiting an answer that actually made sense.

"Because he was my brother," Ulrich stated, nonchalant and apathetic. "Seth and Cabel are my younger brothers. Half-brothers actually," he clarified. "We have the same mother, different fathers."

A wave of panic came over me, prickling my skin at the fingertips. I could feel the quickening pulse in my neck. Something wasn't right.

"Now, I can assure you that Seth will be convicted and sentenced to serve time in prison for what he's done," Ulrich informed me, though his eyes were fixed on a melting cube of ice at the bottom of his glass. "I just wish that we had gotten here sooner."

"I don't understand." Ulrich lifted his head at the sound of my voice. "Why would Seth kill Cabel? His brother. His *twin* brother." I shook my head. "It just doesn't make any sense to me. They're family."

"Why did Cain kill Abel?" Ulrich cleverly responded, noticing the distant, yet ever-present worry in my eyes. I turned my head away and swallowed. "But aren't you pretty familiar with that, Finley?"

"Familiar with what?" I asked, purposely abrupt.

"A family where murder and betrayal are present," he revealed. My eyes widened at the realization of what he knew. "Your father's still on death row, isn't he?"

"I don't have a father," I snapped, as Ulrich ripped my old wounds apart.

Unfazed by my remark, Ulrich leaned towards me from the couch and took my hand in his. "What if I told you that I could get your father off death row, so long as you keep all that you have seen over the past few days a secret?"

I snatched my hand from Ulrich's grip, then slapped my palms together, nervous and taken aback. It felt like the rug had been pulled out from under me.

"If you'd done your research, then you would know that I'm the one who put him there," I confessed, for the sheer sake of testing his ignorance.

"I know you are, dear," Ulrich said, his words nearly believable, if not for the term of affection he had used for me. "But after all these years, you don't want to make amends with your father?"

Taking offense, I slouched back in my chair and scowled. It was my business, my family, my life, and I didn't want to talk about it.

"What is this?" I mercilessly accused. "A bribe?"

Ulrich merely smiled, the green in his eyes twinkling. He was amused.

"I'm only looking to accommodate you, Finley," Ulrich said. "With the election coming up in November, I can't have any bad press." He paused, holding his mouth in an attractive, yet stern manner. "I can't afford any bad press. Do you understand?"

"No," I griped, "I don't."

Annoyed, Ulrich took a deep breath, then sighed. "Imagine what would happen in the polls, if anything about the past few days leaked out.

What if the general public discovered that my kid brother was a convicted murderer with ties to a deadly terrorist organization? I'd lose the election for sure!"

In that moment, I almost wanted to laugh in his face. For someone who hadn't even won the nomination yet, I found it awfully conceited of Ulrich to feel so secure in his presidential prowess. I was over eighteen, but I certainly wasn't voting for Blain Ulrich — that is — if his name even made it on the ballot.

"To be an older brother, you sure don't seem too upset about the fact that Cabel is gone." I withheld my tears, though they threatened to pour from my eyes. I wasn't ready to admit it yet.

Cabel couldn't be dead.

He just couldn't.

"Or the fact that Seth will be going to prison because of it," I carried on. "What kind of brother are you?"

For a solid minute, no one said a word. Even Monty stayed as quiet as a mouse, perhaps too afraid to provoke either one of us further. When Ulrich offered a noticeably crooked smile, I couldn't help but squirm.

"We're a lot alike, you know," he admitted, though I hardly agreed. "One family member murdered. The other sent off to prison for the murdering." Ulrich scanned the length of my face, trapping me with his green-gold glare. "I'm just trying to offer you the closure that you never received as a child. The closure that you should have received as a child," he reiterated.

"I don't need closure," I growled at him, grinding my teeth together to keep from jumping out of my chair and strangling him.

"Well," he exhaled, relenting, "I guess we're done here." Ulrich stood up and towered over me, his eyes flickering from my injured foot to the displeased expression on my face. "Would you like anything else before we take you home?"

Home, yes. Please take me home, so I can cry and suffer and mourn in a place where no one else will see.

"No," I murmured, refusing to let my eyes water in front of him.

"You don't want to see Cabel one last time?" Ulrich grabbed my chin and tugged it upward, forcing me to look into his eyes. I spotted shades of envy around the edge of his pupils. "I know what he meant to you."

Mortified, I glanced over at Monty, then returned my eyes to Ulrich and stared. They didn't wait for a verbal answer. Instead, Ulrich jerked me out of the chair, grabbed my elbow, and steered me towards the nearest door.

Frightened, I looked back over my shoulder at Monty. He held up his hands and mouthed, "It's okay." Then, in a gesture I would never forget, Monty patted the front pockets of his pants, as if I would interpret his cryptic signal as good luck.

Ulrich opened the door and pulled me down

the long corridor, not minding my inability to walk properly on a broken foot. When we reached the last door on the left, Ulrich opened it and pushed me across the threshold.

"Go on," he goaded, his face full of anger and hatred. "My brother's waiting for you."

Ulrich flashed his fake, political smile one last time, and then slammed the door shut behind me.

Chapter 17

On edge, I took a hesitant step forward and surveyed an old, dusty locker room with cool, gray linoleum floors. There was a table in the center of the room that reminded me of something a doctor would use for medical procedures and surgeries. Cabel lay on the table with his arms at his sides, dressed in the same clothes that he had been wearing earlier today. He didn't move.

At first, I didn't want to come any closer. I was too much in shock, in suffering, in denial. But I wouldn't be able to see him when Ulrich returned to take me away. So, I recognized the opportunity for what it was. A visitation. And my last chance to say goodbye.

"Cabel," I sobbed, shortening the distance between us. Tears sprung from my eyes, leaking out like morning dew. "I'm sorry, Cabel." I walked around to the left side of the table and placed my fingers on the edge, near his arm. "I'm so sorry," I cried.

My vision turned blurry, as I stood there beside him. His eyes were closed, but his chest wasn't moving. I remembered the first time that I had seen a body so calm, so still, so at peace with the world. Shaking off the memory, I lifted my hand and touched the side of Cabel's face. He was cold.

My eyes drifted to Cabel's white dress shirt, now soiled with my tears and his blood. The fabric remained open, exposed, just as I had left it. No one had bothered to re-button his shirt, cover up the bullet holes, or clean his bloody skin. Disgusted with Ulrich's idea of family values, I took it upon myself to do what no one else had. Cabel deserved to look closer to the way he once had, whenever Ulrich decided to send his body off and prove Seth's status as a murderer. For Ulrich, that's all Cabel was: evidence.

Choking back tears, I grabbed Cabel's shirt near the collar, peeled it back over his left shoulder, and then tugged the sleeve down over the top of his arm. Most of his skin was unmarked by blood or injury, hidden beneath the cover his shirtsleeve had provided. While I gazed down at Cabel's flawless left arm, something struck me as odd.

Hadn't Cabel been shot in his left arm? Right at the top of his bicep? My mind flashed back to campus, when Cabel had referred to the bullet hole as a mere "flesh wound," and the cabin, where I had watched him pour whiskey onto the same exact spot. Second-guessing myself, I pulled his right shirtsleeve down and searched for the mark, but once again, there was no bullet hole.

All of the blood drained from my body. I took a step backwards, though kept my eyes on the top of his left arm. Was I going crazy? The bullet hole couldn't have simply just disappeared. Could it?

A sudden, banging noise startled me, as I turned around and braced myself. There was a door at the back of the room, between two separate sections of lockers, and that is where the noise was coming from.

Terrified, I swallowed every last ounce of fear and forced it down my throat. I felt everything inside of my body willing me to stop, willing me to stay back, willing me to keep my distance. But I ignored my frantic pulse and crept closer. I had to know what was behind that door.

The banging persisted, as I lifted my hand to the knob, and then began to slowly twist the handle. When I opened the door and looked inside, a man sat tied to a chair with his hands behind his back and his mouth sealed with tape.

I knew that he was a twin. I just didn't know which one.

"Who are you?" I demanded, holding the door open, while I kept most of my body weight on one foot. He yelled at me through the tape and squirmed in the chair, struggling and jerking about. I couldn't understand a single word he said, so I removed the tape and stuck it on the door frame.

"Ow!" he griped, glaring at me with his ice blue eyes. "That hurt!"

"Who are you?" I snarled, tired of waiting for an answer.

His eyes turned soft, as he looked up at me with patience. "Finley," he pleaded. "Come on. It's me."

Dissatisfied, I grabbed the top of his shirtsleeve and jerked it down, exposing his left bicep. There was a strip of gauze tied around his arm, where the bullet hole should have been, but that wasn't enough.

"What are you doing?" he complained, fear and misunderstanding taking shape in the expression on his face.

I ignored him and unraveled the gauze around the middle of his bicep. And there it was. Cabel's unmistakable wound. The bullet hole.

"Finley?"

I felt Cabel's eyes on me, but didn't want to move. For the first time, I noticed his new, clean clothes. A thick, dark green sweater with long sleeves and a simple pair of blue jeans.

Cabel was here.

Cabel was alive.

"Finley, what's wrong? What is it?" Cabel sympathized.

Voiceless, I retied the gauze around his bicep, securing it in place, then pulled his shirtsleeve back over his shoulder.

"Hey," Cabel muttered. "What's wrong?"

I sat down in his lap and pressed my palm against his cheek, letting the stubble of his beard tickle my skin. "I thought you were dead," I whispered, peering at him from underneath my lashes.

Cabel gazed up at me and sighed, a warm, gentle sigh that caressed my lips. "Well, I'm not," he stated, the tone of his voice hinting that he was ready to move on to something else. "Finley?"

"Yes," I breathed, drinking him in.

"Can you untie me please?" Cabel smirked. I wanted to kiss him, but smiled instead.

When I climbed out of his lap, Cabel looked past me, and the expression on his face turned dark. I followed his gaze and saw where his calm blue eyes had landed.

"I'm sorry, Cabel," I said, resting my hand on his shoulder. "I thought he was you."

Cabel gritted his teeth, as his jaw became taut, solid, stiff. Water glazed over the surface of Cabel's eyes, though he blinked away the tears. "Can you untie me please?" he yelled, startling me into submission.

Compliant, I knelt down and untied the rope around his legs, arms, and torso. When I was done, Cabel stood up, and then kicked the chair to the ground. I misunderstood his aggression, until I saw the handcuffs around his wrists.

"Will you get these off me?" he barked, struggling with his hands behind his back.

"Cabel," I softly apologized, shaking my head. "I don't know how. I don't have the..." I drifted off, suddenly remembering the way Monty had patted the front pockets of his pants. My eyes widened, as I beamed at Cabel with delight.

"Well, what?" he snapped.

I stuck my hands into the front pockets of my jeans and felt a wave of energy flood through me. Digging my fist deeper into my right pocket, I clutched the tiny piece of metal into the palm of my hand. I had the key.

"How did you get that?" Cabel asked, as I showed it to him.

"Monty must have put it there. He gave me these clothes."

"Good," Cabel replied. "Try it." He turned around, and I fit the key into the first handcuff, and then the second. In no time at all, Cabel was free.

"Finally," Cabel breathed. He took the handcuffs and the key, casually slipping them into his pocket. Then Cabel pulled me into his embrace and held me close. "I'm sorry you had to see all of this," he whispered in my ear. When I didn't respond, Cabel leaned back and grabbed my hand. "Let's go."

As we walked past a row of lockers, I tightly clenched Cabel's hand, waiting for the other shoe to drop. Before we could reach the exit, a cloud of smoke entered beneath the door. Panicking, Cabel twisted the doorknob to no avail, then shouted and cursed aloud, though I saw no point in screaming. We were trapped.

Chapter 18

Cabel beat his fist against the door. "Blain, let me out of here!" he exclaimed, knocking until his knuckles were bloody.

Meanwhile, the cloud of smoke grew thicker and wider, spreading across the length of the floor. I sank to the ground and started coughing, while Cabel mercilessly slammed his body into the door. But it wouldn't budge.

More smoke billowed out from the air conditioning vents in the ceiling, and before long, I could hardly see anything but clouds of gray. Cabel knelt down on the floor and grabbed my shoulders. "Finley, wake up! Come on. Don't quit," he commanded.

My head lolled back against the wall, as I felt my eyelids growing heavy. "No way out," I mumbled. "There aren't any windows."

Cabel rose to his feet and disappeared into the fog. I thought I heard him talking to someone, saying how sorry he was. But then he returned just as quickly with a red, hostile temper.

"Move, Finley! Move!" Cabel snatched me up off the floor and tossed me over his shoulder, then set me down in front of the lockers on the other side of the room.

Through the haze, I could barely make out the image of Cabel, dragging the table across the floor. At that moment, I realized who Cabel had been talking to. Before moving the body, Cabel must have spoken his final words to Seth.

I held my hands over my ears and flinched, as Cabel repeatedly pounded the table into the door. I could feel the smoke seeping into my lungs, poisoning me, killing me, to the point that I didn't even notice when the sound stopped.

"Finley, come on!" Cabel agitated, dragging me to my feet. "We have to get out of here!" He tugged at my wrist, pulling me after him. But the pain in my foot had returned, and I couldn't bear to walk on it any longer.

"Ah!" I moaned, collapsing to the ground. Cabel picked me up and carried me out of the locker room, through the doorway, and into the hall, where the smoke had collected into a larger mass of toxic fumes.

When we reached the end of the hallway, the door was undoubtedly locked. Cursing aloud, Cabel set me down on the floor, and then kicked the door in with every bit of strength he had left. Soon, I was back in Cabel's arms, as he took me into the main room, at the heart of the fire.

Violent flames consumed the area, turning furniture and adornments to ash. I looked over at the bar, which had now become a fiery blaze, and wondered how much of his precious Scotch Blain had used to start the fire in the first place. Once the ceiling began to crumble, Cabel set me down on my feet and threw what was left of a chair through the window. Glass shattered into tiny fragments on the floor, but Cabel wasn't wasting any time.

"Come on!" he shouted, forcing me towards the window. I felt the heat of the flames, as we dodged falling pieces of drywall. Before I could protest, Cabel grabbed my waist and shoved me through the window, feet first.

I landed on my right foot and cried out in pain, gripping my leg with my hand. Cabel jumped out the window next, and then latched on to my arms, trying to help me to my feet. "Come on, Finley," he pressed. "You have to get up."

Struggling to survive, I got on my knees, as Cabel took my hand. I planted my left foot firmly on the ground, but when I tried to do the same with my right foot, a sharp, bone-shattering pain pierced through me.

"Ah!" I yelled in tortured affliction.

Finally realizing the true nature of the situation, Cabel tossed me over his shoulder again. Only this time, he took off running. We had traveled about a quarter of a mile when the entire building exploded. I lifted my head and watched the beastly orange flames flick and slither throughout the house. The light from the fire lit up the otherwise black, starless sky.

Cabel never stopped to look over his shoulder and watch the building burn to the ground. Instead, he just kept running, until the smoke became a speck of dust in the distance, that even I hardly recognized.

Eventually, Cabel slowed his pace to a walk, before gingerly setting me down on the forest floor. He placed his hands on his hips, gazing back at the direction we had just left, as he caught his breath. The throbbing pain in my foot had transitioned to a dull ache, somewhat similar to the night Cabel had re-broken the bone. I could handle it.

Glancing up at Cabel in the moonlight, I noticed that his face, neck, and hands were covered in soot from the fire. His blonde hair even looked dark, almost black, since it was coated with the same dirty substance. Right then, I decided that I wasn't going to utter a single complaint, regarding my foot, for the rest of the night. Cabel had risked his life for me again. We both could have died in that fire.

"We can stay here for the night," Cabel suggested, nodding at the deer stand in front of him. Lost in thought, I hadn't even noticed the enclosed structure up above, so I lifted my eyes to what looked like a miniature shed on stilts. "I'll go up first and check it out," Cabel volunteered, approaching the tall wooden ladder.

Pulling my knees into my chest, I turned my head away and bit down, deep into my tongue. I could feel my foot swelling, but didn't want to look at it.

"It looks fine," Cabel said, his sudden voice frightening me. I looked up to find him at the entrance of the deer stand, leaning over the edge to talk to me. "You can come up."

I glared up at him with my big, brown eyes. If Cabel expected me to get inside of that tree stand, then he was going to have to provide some assistance. "I can't walk," I reluctantly admitted.

"And I can't carry you," Cabel countered, hanging on to the wooden paneling as he spoke.

"What?" I watched my breath leave my mouth, just as fleeting as the comfort in Cabel's words.

"That ladder's too old," he explained, pointing down below. "It's unstable. If I tried to carry you, there's no way it could take the weight of both of us. Do you think you could climb up on your left foot?" Cabel stared down at me, waiting for an answer. He was serious.

"I guess so," I muttered.

Beyond my limits of exhaustion and fatigue, I somehow managed to muster up enough strength to hop all the way to that deer stand on one foot. How I did that, I'll never know. But when I reached the ladder, Cabel cheered me on, truly believing that I could make it to the top without his help.

Careful, I eyed the rickety, wooden steps of the ladder, and then glanced up at Cabel. He was still waiting, patient man that he was. Holding on to either side of the ladder, I placed my left foot on the lowest step and let my right foot hang down, dangling just above the ground.

"Come on, Finley. You've got it," Cabel encouraged. I maintained my balance and exhaled, already wanting to quit. I didn't have the energy or strength, but Cabel didn't care.

Sluggish, I moved my foot to the next step, as I held on to the ladder for dear life. By the time I reached the middle of the ladder, my arms were screaming in pain.

"You can do it," Cabel assured me. "Come on. You're almost there."

With a deep breath, I pulled my body up, struggling my way to the top. At the last step, I slammed my foot down, pressing all of my weight into that one piece of wood.

"Come on," Cabel repeated, extending his hand for me to take.

I smiled in relief and reached out for his hand. But before I could grasp it, the wooden step beneath my foot gave way and crashed to the ground. Cabel grabbed both of my wrists, while my feet dangled over the steep drop below. "It's okay," he rasped. "I've got you."

Cabel pulled me over the ladder and into the deer stand, gingerly bringing my feet through the opening. With my weight on his body, I closed my eyes and tried to relax, trusting Cabel to hold me upright. After he did, I sat with my back against the wall and my legs straight out in front of me.

Cabel sat down beside me and placed his arm around my shoulder, as I leaned my head against the side of his neck. I felt Cabel's hammering pulse through his throat. A sense of comfort warmed through me, as I realized what that meant. When I slipped on the ladder, it had scared Cabel, too.

"I'm sorry about your brother," I whispered. Cabel stiffened beside me, and I wondered if he knew which one I was talking about.

"Seth was a fun person to be around," Cabel reflected.

"Were you close?" I murmured, keeping my voice down. I didn't want to push Cabel, but felt that he needed to get at least some of what had happened off his chest.

"Not really," he replied. "Maybe when we were kids." Cabel turned his head and gazed down at me. "I don't want to talk about my brother right now."

"Okay," I breathed, noticing his eyes on my lips. Cabel pulled his arm away from my shoulder, and then angled his body towards mine. When he took my face in his hands, I stared into a pair of cool, striking eyes. They were the perfect shade of blue.

As I held my breath, Cabel lowered his face to mine and tenderly brushed his lips over my mouth. Reeling back, I closed my eyes and let Cabel take over, as he kissed me again. I weaved my fingers through the ends of his hair and pulled him towards me, until Cabel touched his lips to the base of my throat. I let out a strangled sigh, while Cabel's mouth traveled to the top of my neck, where my jawline eagerly awaited his touch. When Cabel found my mouth again, I dug my fingernails into the back of his neck, and he groaned.

Awakened by the sound of his desire, I grasped the hem of Cabel's shirt and placed my knees on either side of his hips, straddling him. Cabel sat up on the floor and twisted his fingers through my hair, consuming my mouth, as I unraveled at the pleasure.

Greedy, I rocked forward onto my knees and slid my hands beneath his shirt. Cabel moaned into my mouth, as I bunched the fabric of his shirt up to his chest. My eyes caught sight of several long red marks along his abdomen, and I froze in place.

"Cabel," I sympathized, gently pressing my palm over the places where they had beaten him. He held his jaw taut and lovingly looked into my eyes with adoration, so innocent, so sweet. Wanting to ease his pain, I lowered my mouth to his stomach and kissed the red marks. Cabel's torso tensed in reaction, as he placed his hands in my hair.

"You're so young," Cabel murmured, "so beautiful." He ran his thumb over my cheek, sending tingles where his skin met mine. But there was a look of hesitation in his clear blue eyes, and

I couldn't endure it.

Desperate for his love, I leaned forward to kiss Cabel's lips, but he pulled back, denying me access to his mouth. Cabel pulled his shirt down, and then placed my hands in my lap, like I was a little girl in Sunday school. Narrowing my eyes at Cabel, I tried to understand what I had done wrong. Didn't he want me?

"Touch me," I begged, whining like a sick puppy. Cabel slid out from underneath me, and then knelt down on the floor.

"If I touch you," he began, his eyes glazing over the curves of my figure, before returning to my eyes. "I won't be able to stop."

Disappointed, I sat with my back to the wall and crossed my arms over my chest. I cast my eyes down and let my shoulders sag, while I pouted in front of him. Rejection felt worse than I had ever envisioned. I never would have let myself unravel, if I had known Cabel was going to dismiss me.

"I guess I just thought you liked me," I softly spoke.

"I do like you, Finley," Cabel claimed. "A lot. More than you realize." When I refused to look at him, Cabel sat down beside me and yawned. "I'm tired," he said. "Let's go to sleep."

Taking me by surprise, Cabel pulled me into his arms, and then placed my head in his lap. The gesture reminded me of the way I had fallen asleep as a child, in my father's lap, when he had actually cared. Cabel combed his fingers through my hair, moving every fallen strand out of my face, while my eyelids grew heavy. My breathing slowed, and I fell into a calm, restful state of sleep, where I dreamed of a spiritual, glowing apple tree.

Chapter 19

I felt cool metal slide against my wrist, rudely waking me from a peaceful slumber. Grumpy, I opened my eyes and found Cabel handcuffing my right hand to the thin wooden railing over my head. "Cabel, what are you doing?" I yelped, squirming beneath him.

"You have to stay here," he instructed.

"What? Why?" I searched his face, so wholly and utterly confused. "Where are you going?"

"Promise me that you won't leave," Cabel demanded, his blue eyes alert and focused.

"How can I?" I snipped, banging my metal-clad wrist against the wall.

"Good." Cabel smirked, taking delight in my sarcasm. "You'll be safe here."

As Cabel turned towards the exit and stuck his foot through the opening, I griped in protest. "Please don't go," I begged, feeling abandoned. "What if I never see you again?"

Cabel turned back to me and sighed, then came close enough to plant his mouth on mine. With my free hand, I grabbed the collar of his shirt and molded our lips together, eliciting a deep, husky sound in his throat. Cabel traced the edge of my jawline with his fingertips, kissed me like he wouldn't ever be able to again, and then pulled away. When I opened my eyes, he was gone.

"Cabel," I called after him, knocking the metal handcuff around my wrist against the railing. "Cabel!"

After what felt like an hour, I grew tired of yelling his name and dozed off into an uncomfortable nightmare. I woke up trembling, wanting to extract the painful dream from my memory. But then Cabel appeared at the top of the ladder, and I couldn't help but welcome the relief.

"You're back," I whispered, noting the austere blackness in his eyes. "What's wrong?"

"Blain's dead," Cabel revealed, gloomy as ever. "Monty killed him."

"What? Monty killed Blain? Why?" I watched Cabel, as he unfastened the handcuff around my wrist. The look on his face gave nothing away. He was utterly impassive.

"Because he tried to kill me first."

"Who? Blain?" I searched Cabel's eyes, but could not get them to meet mine.

"Yes," he hissed, impatient.

"Come on. We have to go."

Cabel pulled me to my feet, and then returned to the ladder. I leaned into his side, desperately seeking relief from the pressure on my foot. It was throbbing again, though the discomfort had never really stopped.

"Do you think you could jump?" Cabel asked. He pointed into the wilderness, as I nearly lost my breath.

"What?" I snapped, loathing the direction our conversation had taken.

"I don't think it's safe for you to climb down on one foot, and you know I can't carry you on that ladder," Cabel explained. He tucked a lock of hair behind my ear, gently caressing my cheek in the process.

"So, naturally, I would have to jump out of a building? How many times have we done this now?" I crossed my arms over my chest, determined to find another way.

Cabel turned around and stepped onto the ladder. "Don't worry. This time, I'll be at the bottom to catch you," he said.

I stuck my head through the entryway and kept my eyes on Cabel, until his feet touched the ground. When they did, I felt a wave of nausea form and collect in the pit of my stomach. I didn't want to do this.

"Come on, Finley," Cabel pressed, staring up at me from down below. "I promise," he vowed, "I'm not going to let you fall."

Seething, I listened to the sound of my pulse loudly throbbing in my ears. Since there was no point in delaying the inevitable, I took a deep breath and jumped. Adrenaline coursed through me, as I fell into the open, endless air. When Cabel caught me in his arms, I could hardly believe it. He placed me on the ground, letting me lean into the weight of his body, while I struggled to balance on one foot.

"Climb onto my back," Cabel ordered. "We have to go."

And so, I traveled through the forest with my arms around Cabel's shoulders and my legs in the support of his hands. We kept quiet, watching the sunrise, as streaks of soft orange and golden pink emerged through the trees. I rested my head in the space beside Cabel's neck, while my thoughts drifted back to my father, and all of the times he had carted me around on his back in my youth.

Why hadn't that been enough? Why hadn't I been enough to make him stay? To keep him from changing? Why hadn't he cared enough to love me more than the bottle in his hand?

When I noticed smoke in the distance, my mind returned to the present, as Cabel carried me on his back, until we reached the house, or what was left of it. Monty stood before the ash and rubble, looking like he had been waiting for us longer than he would have liked. Cabel released my legs, and I dropped down onto my left foot, while he kept a firm grip around my waist.

"Where's Blain?" Cabel wondered, scanning the stretch of wilderness surrounding us. I wrapped my arm around Cabel and held him close. If Blain was really dead, then where was his body?

"We were about to bury him, but we've been waiting on you," Monty answered, his eyes on Cabel. Indecisive, Cabel turned his head towards me and placed his hand on my shoulder. I gazed into his eyes, willing him to read my mind.

"Cabel, let's go," Monty growled, making me feel threatened.

"No," I protested. "I want to see the body."

Cabel cocked his head to the side and grimaced. "Finley," he breathed.

"Let her come," Monty said, gesturing towards the trees with his hand. "We don't have much time."

Cabel and I followed Monty away from the rubble and ash, eventually stopping amongst a gathering of pine trees. There was a large rectangular hole dug out in the earth, and Blain's body lay beside it. Cabel grabbed my hand as we approached, his blood turning cold. The two men who had led Cabel to the house in handcuffs yesterday stood at the base of a pine tree. Each of them had a shovel in hand, and they were both wearing gloves.

Cabel stepped closer and let his eyes glaze over Blain's cold, pale, lifeless corpse. He squeezed my hand, while I held my breath, trying not to vomit here, in front of everyone. Tears filled my eyes as I buried my face in Cabel's chest, welcoming his arms around my back.

"Take her to the car, Cabel," Monty suggested.

I felt Cabel's hand move, as he caught the keys that Monty had thrown his way. "We're leaving soon anyway." Cabel slipped the keys into his pocket, and then lifted my chin with his fingers. With my back to Monty, I glanced up at Cabel through a pair of blurry, tear-filled eyes.

"Blain killed Seth, didn't he?" I whimpered, unable to separate myself from my emotion.

"Yes," Cabel hissed.

"And he tried to kill you?"

"Yes." Cabel held my face in his hands, keeping his eyes on me.

"Why?" I demanded. Cabel looked away, and his hands moved to my neck. "Blain mentioned something about political secrets. Is that what all of this is about?" I sobbed. "Is that why he tried to kill you?"

"Don't tell her, Cabel," Monty interrupted, causing Cabel to avert his gaze. "You'll regret it if you do."

"Come on," Cabel said, nudging my arm. "Let's go."

He picked me up and carried me back to the car, while I felt like a child, peeking over her father's shoulder, watching what she has repeatedly been told not to. They tossed Blain's body into the hole, and then shoveled the dirt in afterwards, covering him with soil.

When we reached Monty's car, Cabel sat me down in the backseat, and then climbed in beside me. After shutting the door, he turned his body towards mine and stared. I furrowed my brow, looking on with concern, until he finally spoke up.

"Blain was born in Greece," Cabel confessed.

"What?" I replied, jerking my head in his direction.

"My mother went to Europe one summer during college, and she met a man there. They fell in love, but he was a priest. When she found out that she was pregnant, he abandoned her. She stayed in Greece until the baby was born, and then flew back home. She never saw him again."

I opened my mouth to respond, but Cabel continued before I could say anything.

"Mom raised Blain by herself, until she met my father. Then they got married and had me and Seth. But she never told anyone about what happened in Greece," he hesitated, "except for the four of us." Cabel counted each name off on his fingers, like he was in the middle of a lecture. "Me, Seth, Blain, and my father."

My head was spinning, as I tried to grasp all that Cabel had shared. Insistent, he grabbed my shoulders, and then twisted his fingers through my hair. Cabel was talking too fast, and wouldn't stop, even though I could hardly keep up.

"Finley," he urged, startling me. "My parents died in a plane crash six months ago."

I swallowed, unable to blink beneath Cabel's arctic blue eyes. "Cabel, what are you saying?"

"Blain was never eligible to run for president. He wasn't born here."

"Then how did he?" I countered.

"By bribing politicians and killing everyone who knew the truth."

"Except for you."

Monty knocked on the window behind Cabel, as I gasped aloud. Cabel cursed under his breath, then turned to look through the glass and acknowledge Monty's presence. When Cabel opened the door, I donned the most convincing poker face that I could muster.

"It's time to go," Monty announced. He held out his hand until Cabel gave him the car keys. "Did you tell her?" Monty asked, as if I wasn't sitting right there beside Cabel.

"No," I piped up, leaning over Cabel's shoulder to stare at Monty. "Cabel said that you were going to tell me everything. He said you promised." Monty glowered at Cabel, who shrugged his shoulders apologetically. "Well, are you going to tell me or not?" I cornered, playing my part.

Monty scoffed, and then loudly slammed the car door. As he walked around to the driver's side, Cabel smirked. "You're not a bad liar."

I kept my eyes straight ahead and muttered, "When I have to be."

Monty got in the car, shut the driver's side door, and then looked back at the two of us. "Nothing happened in these woods," he began, pointing to the trees. Then he looked at me and said, "You don't know me. I don't know you.

Cabel is just an old friend of mine. Understood?"

I pursed my lips, teasing Monty, making him wait. "What happened, Monty?" I tried my best to corner him, reeling him in with my big, brown eyes. "Tell me," I commanded. "You promised you would."

"I didn't promise you anything," Monty corrected. "Your boyfriend here did that."

"He's not my boyfriend," I reluctantly admitted.

"What are you doing, Cabel? Messing around with this girl? They'll fire you if anyone finds out. Do you want to lose your job? Ruin your career? Everything you've worked so hard for? For her?" Monty jabbed his thumb at me as he spoke, once again, acting like I wasn't there. "She's not worth it."

"Hey!" Cabel shouted, his pupils dilating at the center. "What happens between Finley and me is none of your business. Now drive!"

Monty glanced from my eyes to Cabel's, then turned around in his seat and started the car. After his diverting outburst, I knew that Monty wouldn't question whether or not Cabel had told me about Blain. But none of that seemed to matter now. All I could think about was how Cabel was going to act when we got back, when I was still his student, and he was still my professor.

Chapter 20

On the way home, I fell asleep in Cabel's arms to the sound of him arguing with Monty. Despite everything that had happened over the past several days, I felt safe. Cabel had done everything in his power to keep me out of harm's way, and I couldn't remember the last time someone had done that for me.

When we reached campus, Cabel woke me up, gingerly holding my shoulders as I lolled my head back against his chest. "We're at school," he whispered in my ear. I shut my eyes and smiled, cherishing the close proximity of his body to mine.

"Is she awake yet or not?" Monty growled from the front seat.

"Shut up," Cabel snapped back, silencing Monty. "Where's your car?" Cabel asked, tilting my chin up to meet his face.

Groggy, I opened my eyes and looked out the window. The sky had turned black while I was asleep, the moon and stars already situated in the night tapestry up above. I held onto Cabel's forearm and sat up in the backseat, rubbing the sleep from my eyes.

"It's in the parking garage," I answered, unable to keep from yawning.

"Which one?" Monty barked, as Cabel's body stiffened in response.

"Behind the psychology building," I mumbled. "But I don't have my keys."

"Where are they?" Cabel inquired.

"In my bag. But I left it in the room where you took me for the experiment."

Monty interpreted my words as a green light and stomped the gas pedal, speeding through campus until we reached the psychology building. When he pulled up in front of the entrance, I unfastened my seat belt and prepared to climb out after Cabel, but he stopped me.

"No," Cabel insisted. "Stay in the car. I'll be right back." He squeezed my arm, and then hopped out of the car, gently shutting the door behind him.

I watched him scale the concrete steps that led to the front door, until he disappeared into the building. Frustrated, I let out a deep sigh and glanced down at my broken foot. Of all the times I hadn't been able to walk, this one aggravated me the most.

"Finley," Monty called, his body still facing the front windshield. "I wanted to apologize."

"For what?" I relaxed into the middle seat in the back, surprised that he was even speaking to me.

"For what I said earlier," he replied, "about

you." Monty's eyes found mine in the rearview mirror, and then darted away to scan our surroundings.

I sat still and folded my hands in my lap, not saying anything. I didn't know what he wanted me to say. And with Cabel gone, I felt less than comfortable in the car alone with Monty.

"What do you think will happen now?" Monty continued. "You know that there's no way the two of you could ever be together." I watched the front door of the psychology building, desperate for Cabel to walk through it. "If you care about Cabel, then end this, whatever it is between the two of you."

I lowered my eyes to the floorboard, plunging headfirst into denial. Of course I had thought about it. What was going to happen to us? Surely, we couldn't treat each other the way we had been, at least not in front of other people. Now that we were back, what was Cabel going to do?

"You're a nice girl, Finley," Monty complimented, only to slight me with another insulting remark. "But you're not right for Cabel." Monty cleared his throat, as the tone of his voice changed from condescending to reassuring. "In time, you'll see," he proclaimed. "Cabel's not right for you either."

As tears threatened at the corners of my eyes, Cabel opened the back door and climbed inside. "Here," he chirped, tossing my bag into my lap. "Now, what floor did you park on?"

"The third," I whispered.

"Go ahead, Monty," Cabel ordered, only he sounded more complacent than demanding. He shut the door behind him, wrapping his arm around me, as Monty steered the car towards the parking garage. "You okay?" Cabel asked, concerned.

"Yeah," I sighed, forcing a smile. "Just tired."

Cabel pressed his lips together and grinned, believing me implicitly. He put my head on his shoulder and rubbed my back, while I breathed in his familiar, manly scent. I didn't know how many more times I would have the opportunity to do that.

When Monty parked behind my car, Cabel leaned forward, between the front seats, and patted him on the back. "Thanks for everything, Monty," he said. "I don't know what to say about Blain or Seth or Mom and Dad. I just-"

"Just be glad you're alive," Monty interrupted. "Both of you."

Cabel turned back to me and pushed a mess of fallen locks over my shoulder. "Do you have the keys?" he asked. I glanced up at him from beneath my eyelashes, blushing and bashful.

"Yeah." I unzipped my bag, reached inside, and grabbed the keys. After handing them to Cabel, he got out of the car and told me to wait for him. Just as Cabel shut the door, Monty caught my eye in the rearview mirror again.

"Finley," he announced, even though I was

already watching him. "Remember what I said."

"Yes, Monty," I obliged. "I'll remember."

Slipping my bag over my shoulder, I plastered a grin on my face when Cabel came to the door and helped me out. "Take care of yourself, Monty," Cabel chattered.

"You too, Cabel," Monty answered, shifting his gaze to me. "Remember what I said," he mouthed. I nodded my head slightly, so Cabel wouldn't notice, as I wrapped my arms around his neck. He lifted my body out of Monty's car, shut the door, and then carried me for the brief moment it took to reach my car.

Once Cabel placed me in the passenger's seat and fastened my safety belt, I looked back over my shoulder and watched Monty drive away. Cabel walked around the car and slid down into the driver's seat, though my eyes remained on the fading car in the distance. "I'm taking you to the hospital," he firmly declared, placing my key in the ignition, as he started the car.

"What?" I grabbed the seat belt over my shoulder and looked him squarely in the eye.

"How many times have you told me that you wanted to see a doctor?" Cabel stuck his head over his shoulder, as he backed out of the parking spot. When I didn't reply, he gazed down at my foot. "I know it hurts," he claimed, shifting the car into drive. "Just let me help you, Finley." Cabel glanced over me, and then turned his eyes back on the road. "Let me help you while I can."

Sighing, I sank into the passenger's seat and glared out the window. My foot was throbbing again, though I did my best to ignore it. In all honesty, the real, live, bone-shattering pain that would be impossible to ignore was the inevitability of tonight. Because no matter how I tried, nothing could stop the clock from striking twelve, when my fairytale prince would return to his natural form and forget that my glass slipper was waiting for him on the staircase, beneath the moonlight, under the glow of a thousand dying stars.

Chapter 21

B y the time we left the emergency room, it was nearly 1 a.m. Cabel had been more than overprotective, accompanying me to see the doctor, harassing the nurse with questions, and then standing outside the door to the x-ray room, where the nurse insisted he was not allowed. I thought Cabel might break something before we could get out of there. And even though he was the most frustrating, stubborn, impatient man that I had ever known, Cabel knew how to make people listen.

"Don't pull too tight. You're hurting her!" Cabel shouted, pointing at the latest nurse who dared attempting to treat me.

"Cabel, it's fine," I declared, narrowing my eyes in admonishment. "Could you please go wait outside?" I whined, fed up with his catapultic anger. "Please," I begged, pouting until he gave in to my big, brown eyes.

"Fine," Cabel barked. He opened the door, stepped through, and slammed it behind him. The nurse flinched, and then relaxed her shoulders in relief, glad that he was gone. Returning her focus to the boot on my foot, she pulled the last strap in place and exhaled.

"That actually is a little too tight," I mentioned, showcasing my sweetest smile as a peace offering. The nurse loosened the strap, and then readjusted the Velcro until I was comfortable.

"Your boyfriend sure is a piece of work," she remarked.

"Oh," I cackled, brushing the matter off. "He's not my boyfriend." The nurse cocked her head to the side and searched my eyes in disapproval. "I mean, we're just..."

"How long have you known each other?" she pried, while I pondered how much I could safely tell her without exposing the truth.

"Not long," I vaguely replied.

"Well, be careful, honey." The nurse handed me a pair of crutches, while I sat on the edge of the examination table. Though I barely knew her, the look in her eyes made me nervous.

"Why?"

She placed her hands on her hips and leaned in close, lowering her voice. I didn't know if she was going to tell me a secret or scold me for what I had done. Either way, I wanted to listen.

"Because that's the kind of man who'll have you pregnant and barefoot in the kitchen before you even lay eyes on him," she preached, warning me. I averted my eyes and withheld my laughter.

"It's not like that." I offered a knowing smile, but that didn't convince her.

"Isn't it though?" The nurse stared into my eyes with arrogance.

"Why are you telling me all of this?" I exhaled, offended, but curious.

"I'm sorry," she muttered, washing her hands in the sink. "It's none of my business."

"No," I agreed, "it isn't." She dried her hands off with a paper towel, then levelled her eyes at me. I was prepared to defend Cabel in every way humanly possible, but maybe I wouldn't have to.

"He just looks like a heartbreaker is all," she explained, shrugging her shoulders. I turned my head away and wished that I didn't understand. My father had looked like a heartbreaker too.

"Do you have kids?" I wondered, anxious to change the subject.

"Yes," she gushed, "two from each husband."

"How many times have you been married?" I held her gaze, knowing that she wouldn't clam up now. We had already given each other a glimpse into our own individual box of secrets.

"Four," she admitted. "I know plenty about men, honey. I've had my fair share of them." The nurse stepped forward and placed her hand on my shoulder. "But what can I say? Sometimes you marry the wrong guy, but have the right kids."

"Yeah," I responded, connecting with her words immediately.

My father had been the wrong guy.

The proof lay at the bottom of my mother's grave.

* * *

"You okay?" Cabel shifted his eyes back to the road, sensing my inner struggle.

"Yeah," I murmured, "I'm fine." Those were the first words to leave my mouth since we had left the hospital. I couldn't stop thinking about what the nurse had said.

The wrong guy. Maybe there was no such thing as the right one.

"Are you sure?" Cabel brushed his thumb across my cheekbone, his fingertips at my jaw.

"No," I droned. He chuckled, then took my hand in his.

"Did Monty get to you?" When I looked down, Cabel's fingertips were skating over the innermost part of my palm. "Don't let him, Finley," he coaxed, authoritative yet kind. "Besides, it's all over now. Everything's going to be all right."

Cabel pulled into my apartment complex and parked in an empty space. I unfastened my seat belt with a yawn, while he reached for my crutches in the backseat. It felt so strange being back, almost like we were in a dream, and the forest had been our reality.

Walking into my apartment felt just as surreal. All of my belongings remained just as I had left them, quietly untouched. Cabel held the door open for me so I could cross the threshold with my crutches, now that moving around had become a one-legged task. After ambling into the living room, I sat down on the couch and let my crutches hit the floor, too tired to pick them up.

I heard the sound of Cabel locking the door to my apartment, as I slipped my foot out of the boot and stuffed a pillow beneath it on the couch. Exhausted, I lay back and threw my arms over my head, content to be sprawled out on a piece of familiar, comfortable furniture. Before I could close my eyes, Cabel approached with my bag in one hand and my keys in the other.

"Just put them on the bed," I instructed. "Please."

Hoping that I hadn't sounded too domineering, I kept my eyes on Cabel, as he walked into my bedroom and put both items on the bed. He returned with a smirk on his face, though I couldn't understand why. Perhaps he enjoyed the view of my simple, ordinary bedroom, where no man had ever entered before.

"Are you hungry?" Cabel stepped into the kitchen and opened the fridge, squatting down to see what was inside. We had stopped for food only once on the road. I was starving.

"Look in the freezer," I suggested. "There should be a couple boxes of frozen pizza in there."

Cabel shut the door to the refrigerator and opened the freezer, where he found both boxes of pizza. "Which one do you want? Pineapple and ham? Or pepperoni?"

"Both," I said. "Aren't you hungry, too?"

"Yes," he hissed, setting the frozen pizza boxes

161

on the counter to thaw out. I grabbed the remote control and flipped the TV on, changing channels until I found an old rerun of *I Love Lucy*. A painful smile came across my face, as bittersweet as the night would inevitably become.

Restless, I watched Cabel out of the corner of my eye, letting my heart swell with joy, longing, pain. He moved in my kitchen with ease, dropping the pizzas in the oven to cook, as I wondered what I was going to do when he was gone. Surely, Cabel's absence would permeate every square inch of my apartment, my thoughts, my mind, my body, my soul, my nights, my dreams.

As Cabel approached, I pulled myself out of my worried daydream and found him with a plastic bag of ice in his hand. He wrapped the pack of cold cubes in a towel, and then delicately placed it over my elevated foot. "Thanks," I uttered, letting Cabel join me on the couch.

With gentle hands, he took my arms and steered me into his embrace, until my head lay on the pillow in his lap. Cabel combed his fingers through my hair, brushing a handful of dark, fallen strands out of my face. Relaxing, I looked up at him and studied every part of his beautifully structured face, from those glacier blue eyes to his pouty, pillow-like lips. One day, all too soon, I would look back on the memory and recall that for just one night, Cabel Jones had been mine.

"You used to watch this show as a kid?" he asked, his voice soft and patient.

"Yeah," I revealed, "it was Mom's favorite."

My eyes returned to the screen, as Lucy and Ethel lost track of the ever-quickening conveyor belt before them, snatching candies up faster than they could be wrapped. When Lucy resorted to popping the small chocolates in her mouth, Cabel chuckled, a deep, husky sort of laughter that made me tingle all over. I knew that I would miss the way that sounded.

"What happened to your mother, Finley?" Cabel wondered during the commercial break.

"I thought you already knew." I paused, craning my neck around to glance up at Cabel.

He draped his arm over my waist and brushed his thumb along my temple. "No."

"Didn't Monty tell you?" I furrowed my brow, hoping to distract him with the expression on my face. But Cabel kept his eyes on me.

"I want to hear it from you," he pressed.

I didn't want to talk about it, but when Cabel cornered me with his artic blue stare, I didn't seem to have much of a choice. Swallowing, I sank the back of my head into the pillow and closed my eyes. My whole life, I had avoided my past, like it was some sick, evil, poisonous disease that needed to be purged from my body. But the memories haunted me at night, invading my body like a cancer, fraying the edges of my spirit until nothing but gray remained. Perhaps it was finally time to purge and be purged, to cleanse and be cleansed, to extract every toxin that had yet to dissolve.

Maybe I was finally ready to let go.

Interpreting my hesitation as denial, Cabel splayed his fingers along the length of my neck, in an attempt to coax the words out of me. "Tell me," he begged. "Please."

Reluctant, I opened my eyes and ground my teeth together. After contemplating the harm in telling him, I shrugged my shoulders and succumbed. I was ready to be clean again.

"My father was an alcoholic." The first admission felt like slicing open an old, untreated wound that had been given plenty of time to fester and rot. But it also felt good.

"Is that why you hate alcohol?" he mused.

I flicked my dark brown eyes up to Cabel's motionless face. He didn't need a verbal answer.

"That night in the cabin," he explained, "anyone else would have taken the whiskey."

I looked off for a moment, contemplating, as I held on to the last of my inhibitions. My father's face flashed to mind. Images of him shouting, drinking, cursing, pushing, shoving, hurting me, hurting Mommy. They would never go away.

The image of my father standing in her blood.

Standing in my mother's blood.

It would never go away.

"When he would drink," I continued, letting my mind peel back the layers of repressed anguish and suffering. "The alcohol, it turned him into someone else."

Cabel tightened his hold around my waistline,

a protective, welcome gesture.

"Someone mean and violent and jealous," I described, tightly shutting my eyes. "Someone that I didn't know." Reliving the pain nearly made me wince, because it seemed so recent.

The memories felt fresh.

By my eighth birthday, he had become an alcoholic.

By my ninth, he was a stranger.

"Drinking changed him," I confessed.

"What did your mother do?" Cabel gently caressed the space where my neck met my shoulder. In that moment I knew, because I could see it in his eyes. I knew that he cared.

"She tried to leave him," I reflected, "and he killed her."

"Did you-?"

"Yes, I saw," I exhaled, gritting my teeth to keep the tears at bay. "I'm the only one who saw."

"You were the only witness," Cabel noted. "What happened afterwards?"

"Foster care," I admitted, avoiding the details that he was truly after. "Some homes were nicer than others." I deliberately omitted the fact that my father had been sent to prison for second-degree murder and that my mother was given a nice, cold grave with a marble headstone engraved with the words, *Daughter. Wife. Mother.*

"What brought you here?" Cabel said.

"Scholarship," I dully remarked.

"You live alone?" Cabel gestured around the

apartment.

"Yes," I muttered.

"No roommates?" he quizzed, though I didn't mind.

"No roommates," I echoed.

"Ever?" His eyes glazed over my face, but his expression remained the same.

"I'm better by myself," I asserted.

"For now," he countered.

"Always."

The side of Cabel's mouth turned up at the corner, as I failed to ignore his sensual smirk. Just like that, I felt the relentless pull, tugging at my heart, prompting me to get closer to him.

I knew what we had to do. And I knew that it would have to happen tonight.

"You were pretty domineering at the hospital, ordering those nurses around. What was all that about?" I fluttered my eyelashes in an attempt to disguise the pain that was blossoming in my chest. I didn't want to think about it. Tonight was all we had left, and I wasn't going to waste it.

"After the past few days, I guess I just felt overprotective," he revealed.

The oven timer went off, beeping intermittently, as Cabel stood up and trudged into the kitchen to silence the noise. Overwhelmed with hunger, I returned my attention to the TV screen, where Lucy and Ethel were engaged in pleasant conversation. A few minutes later, Cabel approached with a plate full of pizza in each hand.

Widening my eyes in delight, I licked my lips and tried not to salivate in front of him.

Cabel took his seat beside me on the couch and set one of the plates in my lap. Ravenous, I seized a slice of pepperoni pizza and sunk my teeth into the hot, cheesy bread. The temperature burned my tongue, but I hardly noticed. After finishing three slices of the pepperoni, I snatched up a small triangular section of the pineapple and ham. My taste buds rejoiced in delight, as the tropical fruit blended with the overly salted pork to create the perfect combination of meat and tang. I had never been more grateful for prepackaged food in my life.

"You must have been hungry," Cabel quipped.

Glowering into his crystalline eyes, I held the warm plate in my lap and scoffed. Once Cabel finished eating, he collected both plates, washed them in the sink, and then put the bag of ice for my foot in the freezer. I eyed the clock on the wall, loathing that insistent, ticking creature, who had been forever cursed with the boundless task of advancing time, shoving the present into the past, while the future remained two steps ahead of everyone else. Regardless, time had taught me to value the fleeting moments and their precious ephemerality, simply because neither last.

How I longed to stay right there, with Cabel and fruity meat pizza and *I Love Lucy* reruns. They filled my apartment with pink, glowing warmth, as opposed to the dull, dreary grayness that usually permeated the walls, when there was nothing more than textbooks to keep me company.

After the past few days with Cabel, nothing would ever feel like it had before. I couldn't bear the thought of never having his arms around me again. And when he came back to the couch, I couldn't prolong the pain anymore. I was ready, and I wasn't turning back.

Chapter 22

Yawning, I straightened my posture on the couch and stretched my arms out over my head. Cabel picked my crutches up off the floor, extending his hand for me to take, as I placed all of my weight on one foot. With a crutch beneath each arm, I grasped the rubber hand grips and took off, headed towards the bedroom.

Like a faithful guardian, Cabel followed closely behind, even though I had not asked him to. I felt his presence at my back, trailing my footsteps, while I passed through the bedroom and into the bathroom. My blood pulsed loudly in my ears, a persistent, terrifying sort of rhythm that made me tremble. When I stopped at the sink, Cabel caught my eye in the mirror, and I froze.

"What?" He grinned, studying my behavior closely.

"How am I supposed to brush my teeth?" I cleverly diverted.

Falling for my ruse, Cabel took the crutches from me, leaned them against the wall, and then clutched my waist with his hands and lifted me onto the bathroom counter. I felt all of the air leave my lungs, as Cabel stood between my legs, his sultry gaze drifting from my mouth to my eyes. But then he turned to open the medicine cabinet, where he seized my toothbrush and toothpaste from the highest shelf. My cheeks flooded with warmth, while I watched him squeeze a thick strip of blue, minty paste onto the straight, white bristles. When he lifted my chin in the palm of his hand, I closed my mouth and swallowed, letting his delicate touch rush over me.

"Open," Cabel instructed, setting his thumb and forefinger on either side of my jaw. Resistant, I pressed my lips together and shook my head in disapproval. "Finley," he scolded.

The deep, husky tone of his voice stirred something inside of me that had yet to be discovered. Feeling flushed, I smiled at him without showing any of my teeth, teasing him further. In response, Cabel tugged at my chin until my lips separated, allowing him access to my mouth. Without hesitation, he slipped the toothbrush past my tongue and onto my bottom row of teeth, scrubbing in a circular motion from one side of my mouth to the other. When Cabel was finished, he repeated the process on my top row of teeth, his icy blue eyes focused on the task at hand.

"Stick your tongue out," he softly spoke, sending a cool shiver throughout my body. I situated my hands on either side of my hips and did my best Gene Simmons impersonation, while

Cabel dragged the toothbrush over my taste buds. Afterwards, he pulled my hair back, so I could cup my palms beneath the faucet and rinse my mouth out with water in the sink.

"Well," I murmured, patting my lips dry with a washcloth. "That was interesting."

"Better?" Cabel darkly crooned.

I slid my tongue over both rows of teeth, feeling their clean, smooth texture. "Better."

Satisfied, Cabel leaned in and rubbed his nose against mine, as I felt his breath on my face. My mouth fell open, willing and ready to surrender, though I was quivering with fear.

"Do you mind if I take a shower?" he whispered, his lips beneath my ear.

"No," I exhaled, holding on to the counter for support.

Cabel took a small step back, tantalizing me, until he lifted his arms over his head. My heart pounded loudly inside of my chest, as I let my eyes travel from his piercing blue eyes to his full, lush lips. Feeling brazen, I gathered the hem of his shirt with my fingers, then slowly peeled the fabric over his smooth, muscular torso. Cabel tensed at the touch of my nails against his stomach, while I dragged the material over his skin, past his chest and shoulders. When the shirt came over his head, I let it fall to the bathroom floor, and then waited for Cabel to draw near.

Setting his sights on me, Cabel clasped my cheek in the palm of his hand and tucked my brunette locks behind my ear with his fingers. The blacks of his eyes dilated, thinning out the blue, while I endured the warm, burning ache beneath my skin. I felt my chest rise and fall, the closer his body moved towards me, until I could hardly stand the distance any longer.

When Cabel's mouth finally met mine, I couldn't help but whimper. He held my face in his hands, then slowly, mercifully, deliberately pushed my lips apart, as his warm breath rushed in. Hot blood coursed through my veins, awakening my physical urges and desires.

I wanted to be touched. I wanted to be loved.

Alive with fire, I took his face in my hands and planted my mouth on his. I could taste the pizza that we had just eaten, traces of pepperoni and pineapple lingering on his breath, but I welcomed the new taste. Cabel's kisses felt like an electric flame across my body, intended to scorch every nerve ending from head to toe. As his lips moved along my neck, I tilted my head back and sighed, letting the pleasure flood through me.

Craving Cabel's touch, I wrapped my legs around his hips and forced him to come closer. When his teeth touched the edge of my earlobe, I moaned aloud, clinging to him in desperation. Cabel reacted to the sound of my longing and slid his hands beneath my top, letting them dance across my naked back, until he reached the clasp on my bra strap.

I let out a startled sigh, but didn't push him

away.

"Finley," Cabel gasped, panting against my mouth. "We don't have to."

Lowering my eyelashes, I pressed my nose against his cheek and felt his heavy breathing against my tingling skin. My hands lay on his shoulders, as I held my mouth before his, leaving a hint of a kiss on his lips. "All we have is tonight," I whispered.

Cabel pulled away slightly, looking into my young, willing eyes, while a current of emotions flitted across his own. To soothe his frantic mind, I lifted my hand to his face and stroked the stubble of his beard. His nostrils flared in response, his pupils widening further.

"Please don't make me cross a line," he said, catching his breath.

"I thought you already had."

Cabel narrowed his eyes at me and loudly exhaled through his nostrils.

But I had already made up my mind. I knew what we had to do.

Tired of waiting, I forced my mouth against his, as we crashed back into each other. Cabel succumbed to my relentless passion and groaned, reacting to my fingers in his blonde hair. Unable to stand the burning torture anymore, Cabel picked me up and carried my clinging body into the bedroom. Brimming over with desire, I wrapped my arms around him and held on tight.

Cabel laid me down across the bed, with the

pillows to the right of my hand, and then climbed on top of me. I raised my head to dissolve the space between us, as his mouth returned to mine, his knees digging into the mattress on either side of my hips. His fingers tugged at the bottom of my shirt, sending a thrill of rushing emotions across the surface of my skin. When I lifted my arms, Cabel pulled the shirt over my head and tossed it on top of my pillowcase. I closed my eyes and relaxed, relishing the feel of his fingertips, as they softly caressed the inner part of my arm.

His lips blazed a trail around my neck, over my clavicle, down the flat line between my breasts, and then across the bones of my ribcage. Every brush against my skin felt so utterly sensitive, so breathtakingly new, so achingly good, that I balled the bed sheet up in my hand.

Cabel unfastened the metal snap on my jeans, pulled the zipper down, and then grabbed the belt loops, exposing my bare legs. I felt his fingertips glide along the sides of my thighs, as he peeled the skin-tight fabric over my knees, past my calves, and around my ankles. When I heard the jeans hit the floor, Cabel lowered his body over mine and ravaged my lips. I kissed him back with powerful vigor, never taking my mouth from his, even when it hurt.

Holding my wrists over my head, Cabel pinned me beneath him on the mattress, where I gladly wanted to stay, underneath his warm, strong body. When his fingers reached the band at the top of my panties, I clamped my hand around his bicep, and he froze above me.

"I've never done this before," I confessed. "But I'm glad it's with you."

Cabel's eyes widened, as he reeled back and sat on his knees. I smiled to soften the gravity of my words, but Cabel withdrew his hands from my body and stared down at me.

"What do you mean you've never done this before?"

I averted my eyes in embarrassment. There was no need for an explanation.

"I can't do this," Cabel declared.

"What?" I leaned up on my elbows and searched the ever-changing look in his eyes.

"I can't. I'm sorry." Cabel climbed off the bed, walked into the bathroom, and then shut the door behind him. I heard the shower come on, as tears filled my eyes. Tonight was all we had left, and Cabel had squandered it. He had wasted our precious, final moments together.

Crushed, I rolled over on the bed and snatched my shirt off the pillowcase. After collecting the black jeans from the floor, I tossed both garments into the closet, along with my bra. Then I pulled a large t-shirt over my head and hopped my way to the bed, so I could step into my favorite pair of sweatpants. Since my crutches were still in the bathroom, I bounced into the kitchen on one foot and drank a glass of water to numb the pain in my chest, but more importantly, to quell the burning sensation that lingered everywhere else.

On the trip back to my bedroom, I tripped over the threshold and fell to the ground. Crying out in pain, I pulled my foot into my chest, thankful that I hadn't landed on it wrong. Cabel burst out of the bathroom and rushed to my side, kneeling down beside me. In passing, I noticed that he had put the same clothes back on and that his hair was wet.

"What happened?" he yelled, his head shaking with worry.

"I fell! What do you think happened? You locked my crutches in the bathroom!"

"I'm sorry," Cabel breathed.

For the second time tonight, Cabel picked me up in his arms and carried me to the bed. Only this time, he pulled the covers back and tucked me in, like I was a pajama-clad child equipped with a teddy bear and a nightlight. I turned onto my side, rested my head on the pillow, and stared straight ahead, frustrated beyond comparison.

"I feel like a fool," I admitted. The mattress squeaked, as Cabel took a seat on the edge.

"I care about you, Finley," he said, making my eyes water.

The burning sensation in my chest had disappeared, leaving me hollow.

"I'll always care about you." Cabel took hold of my limp hand and twined his fingers through mine. "But I just don't see how we could ever make this work."

Heavy tears streamed down my cheeks, salty and wet. I felt weak, hopeless, useless.

"Don't cry," he pleaded, as if he had a right to. "Please don't cry."

Cabel lifted the covers and slid underneath them, while I remained motionless. I felt his hands around my stomach, as he pulled me into his arms, my back pressed against his chest.

"Please don't cry," he whispered in my ear, his stubbly chin on my shoulder.

"Cabel, I-"

"Don't say it," he hissed, covering my mouth with his hand. "You'll be glad you didn't."

Sobbing quietly, I allowed the pain to spread into my chest, as the numbing ache pierced through me. Cabel withdrew his hand from my mouth and brushed my hair over my shoulder. I felt his knuckles against my throat, tormenting me with the denial of his affection.

"You wouldn't want me, Finley," Cabel insisted, "not if you really knew me."

"But I do know you, Cabel." My voice squeaked with every syllable.

"No, you don't." His breath cascaded down my neck. "You deserve someone better than me."

When I tried to move, Cabel tightened his grip around me, so I couldn't turn my head back to look at him. I hated him for robbing me of what I wanted most in this world. *Him.*

"Sleep," he sighed. "Just close your eyes and

sleep."

Eventually, the flood of tears waned and exhaustion took over. Before drifting off, I braided my fingers with Cabel's, as his arm lay draped over my abdomen. After tonight, we would never sleep beside one another again, so I made the best of our last shared slumber and let him hold me.

When I woke up the next morning, Cabel was gone. But on my nightstand, by the glowing light of my digital clock, sat a perfectly polished, shiny red apple.

Chapter 23

When classes resumed on Monday, I took the bus to campus, unable to drive with my broken right foot. The student body was furious, because Spring Break had been removed from the semester schedule to compensate for the previous week of cancelled classes. The president of the university called the unexpected invasion a "terrorist attack," which now elicited a need for additional security measures.

All I could do was keep quiet and resist the urge to tell my peers what had really happened. That Cabel was all those men had been after. That Blain had devised a plan to eliminate anyone who knew his secret. That I had witnessed all of it and fallen helplessly in love as a result.

Watching Cabel teach felt like a prison sentence. I couldn't focus on the difference between solution-focused therapy and cognitive behavioral therapy, because every time I saw Cabel's mouth move, I remembered exactly where it had been on me. Visions of our last night together flashed through my mind, as I felt heat rush over me.

His lips on my throat.
His hands on my thighs.
His fingers between my breasts.

Before the end of class, I allowed myself one glance at the husky blue gleam in his eyes. Enduring the rest of this semester was going to be a burden that I would have to bear.

I paid Cabel an unexpected visit in his office that afternoon, unable to stay away. Our love may have been doomed from the start, but there was no doubt in my mind that Cabel cared. As long as he loved me, I could ride out these years of stolen glances and hushed affection. If I could endure purgatory long enough, then maybe we could still end up together.

"Well, Miss O'Connell," Cabel drawled "What can I help you with today?"

"How are you?" I asked, desperate to touch him.

"Fine," he curtly replied, his piercing blue eyes stern and guarded.

"I miss you," I bravely revealed.

Cabel stood up, took a handful of long strides, and then closed the door. When he returned to his desk and sat down, I saw the anger in his eyes. But after just one weekend without him, I felt drained of blood, oxygen, life. I had to let him know how I felt.

"Finley," Cabel growled, as if I had committed some cardinal sin. But hadn't he been the one to push me up against a wall? Surely, Cabel had broken just as many rules as I had. "I told you that there's no way this could ever work. Things have to go back to the way they were."

"I don't want them to," I carefully whispered, seeking agreement in his eyes.

"Unless you want to discuss something about the course, I don't think you should come by my office anymore," he said. The look on his face was so cold, so apathetic, so unlike Cabel, that it knocked the breath right out of me. Maybe Cabel had been right that night in my bedroom.

Maybe I didn't know him at all.

"Why?" It was a question that I already knew the answer to, but I had to ask it, if only to buy more time, to lengthen the conversation I had been aching to have with him.

"It will be better for both of us," he assured me, folding his hands together over his desk. "Trust me."

"I do." My eyes bored into his, testing him, pressing him, reminding him. Cabel cast his eyes on the separate stacks of papers on his desk and sighed.

"I have a lot of work to catch up on, Finley." He wouldn't meet my eyes, keeping his gaze down. "You should go home and rest your foot."

In an instant, my hurt turned to rage. While Cabel glanced over the first document, I reached into my bag and grabbed the apple, gingerly placing it on his desk. He froze, set the document aside, and then glared into my provoking eyes.

"Why did you leave that by my bed?" I inquired.

Cabel sucked his cheeks inward, as I observed how tightly he was clenching his jaw. When I saw the pupils of his eyes dilate, relief came over me at the small victory.

So I did still have an effect on Cabel Jones.

"It was a mistake," he said. "Poor judgment on my part. I'm sorry."

I crossed my arms over my chest and glowered. That would not be enough to satisfy me.

"It's just a reminder," Cabel muttered, playing it down.

"Of what?" I tilted my head to the side, providing him with a perfect view of my cold, lonely neck. The same neck that he had molded his mouth to only a few nights ago.

"You're the one thing that I can never have." Cabel glanced down at the apple, and then lifted his eyes to mine. I knew that he wasn't going to touch the piece of fruit, just like he wasn't going to touch me. "Please get out of my office."

Pulling my eyebrows together, I glared at Cabel, and then snatched the apple off his desk. When Cabel returned to his work, so quick to ignore and dismiss me, I raised the apple to my lips and took a big bite. As the fleshy fruit floated in my mouth, I placed the partially eaten apple on the stack of documents and watched juice trickle down, seeping through the pages.

Cabel shut his eyes in frustration and planted

his fingers on his forehead. I left his office without looking back and headed home to eat dark chocolate, watch a sad movie, and cry. Even though the apple had looked sweet, it left a bitter taste in my mouth.

Chapter 24

Weeks passed, as Cabel and I became successful at ignoring each other. When I couldn't stand the burning ache in the pit of my stomach any longer, I met with my academic advisor and used my broken foot as leverage for switching into an online section of clinical psychology. She took pity on me and filled out the form, while I marveled at the speed with which she scrawled her signature in black ink at the bottom of the page.

"Here," she offered, sliding the form across the surface of her desk. "Just make sure you get your current professor to sign this, then I'll help you get enrolled in the online section, since it's so late in the semester."

"Why does my professor need to sign this?" I panicked.

"Because the approval of your current professor is required. He's the one who's been giving you a grade," she reasoned, looking at me like I should have known better.

"Oh." I blanched instead of blushing, a rare occurrence for me, as realization struck. I wouldn't be able to escape Cabel as easily as I had thought.

"Make sure you bring a doctor's note too, whenever you turn the form in. And I hope your foot gets better soon." The advisor waved a small hand in the air, and then returned to typing.

"Thanks." I stood up with my crutches and forced a smile, hoping she couldn't see beneath my mask and discover that the only part of my body that had actually been broken was my heart.

Bones could be mended, but scars never healed.

And so, I found myself in Cabel's office again, sitting at the chair in front of his desk, while he skimmed the form that my advisor had given me. When Cabel finally spoke, his eyes remained on the page in his hand, and his voice turned from hard to abrasive.

"I'm not signing this," Cabel refused, before he was even done reading it.

"Why not?"

"Tell me why you want to drop my class, Finley." Cabel was wearing his reading glasses, the ones that made him look like a young Robert Redford. I loved those glasses.

"I'm not dropping your class," I denied. "I'm switching into an online section."

"If I sign this form, you won't be my student anymore," he elucidated. "That means you're dropping my class."

"I'm lightening my on-campus course load, so

I can spend more time off my foot," I explained, knowing that he would undoubtedly find some inherent contradiction in my words and use it against me.

"Are you dropping any of your other classes?" he probed.

"I'm not dropping anything," I announced, raising my voice.

"I'm sorry," he bitterly remarked. "Let me rephrase the question. Are you switching into any other online sections of your other classes?"

"No."

"Then why did you pick my class?"

"It has nothing to do with your class and everything to do with my foot!" I barked back, my chest rising and falling in reaction to my sudden change in temperament.

"You expect me to believe that?" Cabel leaned back in his chair, and the motion made the seat squeak. "We both know the real reason why you're here."

"Yes, I do," I claimed, ignoring his last remark.

"You do realize that if you switch into an online section, you'll have to start the coursework for the entire semester all over again. All of your hard work would have been wasted."

"Yes, I know."

Cabel ground his teeth together, and then chewed on the edge of his lip, trying to make me reveal my motive for switching classes. But I would never give him the satisfaction.

"Finley, I think you're making a mistake," he advised. "You study hard. You show up to every lecture on time. You do well on exam day. You have the highest average in both sections of my clinical psychology class."

I let my eyes sink to the floor and sighed. Listening to his compliments felt like a knife in my back. Academically, I measured up, but that wasn't enough to garner his love.

"Why would you throw all that way?" he said, irritated.

Because you wouldn't love me when I needed you to.

"Finley," he called, assuming that I had stopped paying attention, even though I was.

I always was.

"This will be better," I professed, throwing his own words back in his face. "For both of us."

Nothing was spoken for a moment, convincing me that I had won. But then Cabel hunched forward and planted his elbows on top of his desk. He wasn't going to budge.

"I'm sorry, Finley but I'm not going to let you-"

"This is what I want," I interrupted. "So please, just sign the form, Cabel."

"This won't make life any easier for you," he noted. "You'll be making things a whole lot harder on yourself." Cabel's tone turned aggressive, yet he failed to corner me.

"I can handle it," I said, convincing Cabel on the spot.

When he touched his pen to the bottom of the form, I could hardly believe it. Cabel held out the document over his desk, as I took it from him with a strange mixture of relief and regret. Now that Cabel had signed the form, how much time would go by until I saw him again?

Why had he let me go so easily? A small voice answered the question in my head.

Because you wanted him to.

"Thank you." I smiled at Cabel, while he twisted the pen in his hand, his eyes downcast and quiet. Saving my tears for later, I stuffed the form into my bag and left before he had the opportunity to change my mind. Later that night, alone in my apartment, I looked at the form for the first time since Cabel had signed it.

Warmth flooded my cheeks, when I realized that Cabel hadn't marked his name or initials down on the paper. Instead of his signature at the bottom of the page, Cabel had inked two letters that would forever represent the way I felt about the death of our newly buried romance.

NO.

Unwilling to yield, I headed to the Registrar's office the very next morning, determined to drop the class. Cabel had considered my switching from his class into an online section as dropping a course anyway, so I might as well at this point. But the Registrar's office would take a whole lot more convincing and swaying, as I soon learned.

"I'm sorry, miss," the older, soft-spoken

gentleman said. "But it's simply too late in the semester for you to drop a class. You should have come by a couple weeks ago. That was the final deadline."

I hadn't expected that response, so I complained of my foot, as I had with the advisor. But the man told me that the only other option was to take a medical leave of absence, which would require me to drop all five classes that I was currently enrolled in. And so, I accepted my fate.

For the rest of the semester, I was stuck in CLP 4671 with Cabel Jones.

Chapter 25

Three more weeks passed, until I was finally able to walk without crutches. My foot felt funny, when I took my first step forward in the boot, stretching and pulling on the inside from lack of use. But I was glad to have a pair of free hands again, as I strolled through campus or walked to the bus stop at the end of the day. It was nice to feel more independent.

In celebration of my newfound freedom, I went to the grocery store and headed to the freezer section. Part of me was scared that I might bump into Cabel. But part of me was also disappointed when I didn't.

The grocery store was sold out of frozen pizza, but not the whole section, just the kind I wanted. Pineapple and ham. Discouraged, I left the aisle and trudged through the fruit department, noticing a large basket of apples on sale. But not all of the apples were on sale.

Just the red ones.

When I arrived back at the apartment complex, I checked my mail, and that's when matters took a turn for the worse. To fund the new, expensive security detail on campus, the university had drastically reduced the amount of money allocated for academic scholarships, including mine.

My heart sank, as I tallied up how much money was left in my savings account from working more days than not during all four years of high school. There was no way I had enough.

What I did have were bills to pay. Rent. Food. Gas. Electric. Car Insurance. Internet. Cable.

I rolled my eyes at the ceiling, as the alternative spelling of that word came to mind. If Cabel and I were still on speaking terms, I could have asked for his advice, and he would have told me the best thing to do. Cabel was rational and shrewd, with more common sense than most people acquired in a lifetime.

I missed him, and I couldn't help wondering if he missed me, too.

By the next weekend, I didn't have to wonder anymore.

For the past week, I had been going to class in the daytime and waiting tables at a local steakhouse at night. The hours were exhausting, but the tips were very generous. And though no one liked to use the phrase, I needed the money.

But that Saturday night, as I carried a tray of drinks across the dining room, my eyes widened in horror, and I felt all of the color leave my cheeks.

Cabel had just been seated at a booth in my section, and he wasn't alone.

He was with another woman.

Chapter 26

Freezing in my tracks, I stopped paying attention to my surroundings and bumped into a table of four elderly women, who most closely resembled the main cast of *The Golden Girls*. The serving tray that I had been carrying crashed into the side of their table, toppled over, and then bathed all four ladies in a blend of Shirley Temples and club soda.

"Ah!" one of the women exclaimed, tossing her small, wrinkled hands in the air. "We're all going to smell like cherries!"

"I'm so sorry," I said, kneeling down to clean up the mess.

"What am I going to do about my hair?" another complained, showcasing her short, russet mop of curls. "I just got a permanent in it yesterday!"

"I'm so, so sorry, ma'am," I apologized. Before I could say anything more, Jeremy appeared beside me with a pair of dish towels in his hand.

"All right, ladies," he cheered. "What can I get you all this evening? Please forgive poor Finley here." He placed his hand on my back. "She's broken her foot and isn't all together these days."

"How did you break it?" the first woman wondered, our earlier scuffle forgotten. I looked up at her in astonishment and blinked, hardly believing that her sour reaction had dissolved.

"I fell down the stairs," I muttered. When none of the women showed any interest beyond that, I wiped the puddles of spilled liquid from the table and kept my eyes down.

"Well, I'm taking care of you gorgeous girls for the rest of the evening. Can I get you a fresh round of drinks?" Jeremy clapped his hands together, energetic and playful.

While he retook their drink orders, I mouthed the words, "Thank you."

He looked me over politely, and then winked.

Clearing the unused glasses away from the table, I felt someone's eyes on my face and looked up. Cabel was staring at me from across the room. My eyes widened, and I retreated to the kitchen in a hurry. Jeremy was right behind me, tugging at my elbow, when I deposited the glasses in the sink. I had never felt so incompetent in my life. It was difficult being the new girl at anything, but most of the other waiters and waitresses could care less about how I was getting along or the fact that my foot was still in a boot.

But Jeremy was sweet. Jeremy was cute. And Jeremy liked me.

"Are you all right?" he asked, leaning against

the counter. I dried off the mess that the drinks had left on my black shirt and apron.

"You're so much better at this than I am."

"It's your first week," he reminded me. "Give yourself a break."

Jeremy had been my favorite from the start. With ginger hair, green eyes, and pale, freckle-covered skin like mine, he wasn't terribly tall, terribly thin, or terribly handsome. But Jeremy was always the first person to ask me how my day was going. He felt like a friend, and I hadn't had one of those in a while.

When Jeremy turned to pick up a selection of entrées from the chef, I grabbed his shirtsleeve and pulled him back. "Do you think you could do me a favor?"

"Another one already?" Jeremy smirked, patting my arm when my face fell. "I'm just messing with you."

"Oh," I exhaled, letting out the breath I had been holding.

"So, what's up?" Jeremy held a round serving tray in both hands, and then lifted it over his shoulder and headed for the swinging door. I followed his footsteps and walked with him into the dining room.

"Do you see that table over there?" I leaned my head towards Jeremy and pointed to where Cabel and his mystery guest were sitting.

"Yeah." Jeremy took a good look, and then shuffled his feet over to a table of two teenage couples on a double date. I helped him serve the entrées, though I'm surprised Jeremy let me after what had just happened.

"I hate to ask you this, but do you think you could go wait on that table?"

Jeremy slid the empty serving tray beneath his arm, holding it against his torso, as he trudged back to the kitchen. "I don't know Finley," he said. We leaned near the swinging door, pressing our backs into the wall. "We're really busy tonight, and I'm already covering a table in your section."

"Please, Jeremy," I begged, grasping the collar of his shirt. "I'll give you half of my tips tonight, if you just do this for me."

"All right, jeez, calm down. What's so bad about that table anyway?"

Shifting my gaze to the floor, I dropped my hands from Jeremy's shirt and crossed my arms over my chest. "I don't want to talk about it."

"Finley, I can't help you if you don't tell me what's going on."

"Okay," I succumbed. "Do you see the guy sitting at that table?"

"Yeah."

I looked down, twisting my fingers together. "Well, he's..." I trailed off, then regained enough composure to form another broken sentence. "It's just..."

"It's okay, Finley," Jeremy sympathized. "I understand."

"You do?"

"Yes."

"Ah," I sighed in relief and gave him a hug. "Thank you, Jeremy."

"I'm not doing this for free," he chuckled. I pulled back, holding him at arm's length.

"You'll get your share of my tips," I promised. "Don't worry."

We parted ways, and then Jeremy talked over his shoulder, "Wasn't gonna."

After passing that table off to Jeremy, relief washed over me. I had gladly bartered a share of my hard-earned cash in exchange for not having to deal with Cabel and his date, girlfriend, mistress, whatever she was. In actuality, I would have given Jeremy all of my tips for the next three weekends, if it meant that I didn't have to face Cabel. If only it had been that simple.

Rushing between tables, I hurried into the kitchen and collected a pair of dessert plates. A thick slice of chocolate cake, oozing with hot fudge and caramel sauce, sat at the center of each. Jeremy caught my arm on the way out and pushed me back into the kitchen.

"Jeremy, what is it?" I put the desserts on the countertop, aggravated that he had almost knocked me over. All I needed was another disaster, where more inventory was sacrificed.

"I can't wait on that extra table for you, Finley. I'm sorry." Jeremy shrugged his shoulders, and then turned to walk away.

"Wait," I cried, grabbing hold of his arm.

"Why not? What happened?"

"That guy?" He cocked his head to the side and rolled his eyes in the direction of the dining room. "The one you showed me."

"Yeah. What about him?" I felt the kitchen walls closing in on me, as I slowly but surely interpreted the look in Jeremy's bright green eyes. My back-up plan wasn't going to work, and I didn't have another one.

"He wants you."

Chapter 27

Yes, Cabel had specifically asked for me to wait on his table, when Jeremy tried to fulfill his end of the bargain. Hot blood rushed to the surface of my cheeks, as the task of breathing became difficult. I couldn't face him. I wouldn't face him. Not when he had pretended that he cared so much. That had obviously been a lie, because now he was here with her.

"Just go on, Finley," Jeremy encouraged, steering me towards the door. "The two of you obviously know each other." I grabbed both pieces of chocolate cake, since he was dragging me away from the kitchen counter. "There's three of them now," he mentioned, "so be on your toes."

"Three of them?" I spun around to face Jeremy, and he nodded.

"Yeah, the woman's husband just showed up."

My jaw dropped, as I rocked back on my heels. "Husband? She's married?"

"Yeah," Jeremy declared. "Go and see for yourself."

Donning a brave face, I stepped into the dining room and dropped the desserts off at another table. Then I made my way to the booth, where Cabel and both of his mystery guests were waiting. When I approached, Cabel turned his head and waved. I wondered what it would take to make him smile.

"Hello," I murmured.

"Finley, this is Nelson and his wife, Pam." Cabel gestured to each of them, respectively. "Nelson was my roommate at Cornell."

"Oh," I inhaled a breath of fresh air, finally understanding. "It's nice to meet you both." I shook Nelson's hand, then Pam's, surprised by how different she looked up close.

With shiny black hair, dark eyes, olive skin, and good bone structure, Pam looked pretty enough to make me feel threatened. But now that I knew she was already taken, my worries dissolved in seconds. Nelson draped a protective arm over Pam's shoulder, perhaps sensing the innate jealousy I had felt towards her earlier.

"Cabel tells us that you're the top in his class," Pam commented.

"Oh?" I didn't know how to respond, too stunned to say anything else.

"Yes," Cabel answered. "She's my best student."

Avoiding his subtle blue gaze, I retrieved a writing pad from my apron and proceeded to take their orders. Jeremy had already delivered their drinks, so that was one less thing to worry about. Even though I had misinterpreted Pam's identity, I didn't feel like dealing with Cabel tonight.

After hours of standing on my feet, the restaurant finally closed, and I couldn't have been happier. People fled through the doors, workers and guests alike, until there was no one left but me and Jeremy. His father owned the place and had always scheduled Jeremy to work until closing. Over the past few nights, I had stayed behind to help him, simply because it was better than returning home to an empty apartment.

"So, how did you do tonight?" Jeremy pulled up a chair and turned it around, so that his hands dangled over the back when he sat down. He was drinking a bottle of beer.

"Not too bad," I remarked, counting the bills one last time, before splitting the money into two equal piles. "Here's your share." Jeremy set his beer bottle down on the table and placed his stack of bills on top of mine. I cocked my head to the side, utterly perplexed by his behavior.

"I don't want your money, Finley," he gently crooned. My mouth stayed open, gaping in surprise. "Besides, you ended up waiting on that table anyway."

"But you filled in for me when I knocked all those drinks over."

"Keep it, Finley." Jeremy placed the money in the palm of my hand and closed my fingers around the bills. "I wouldn't have taken it anyway, even if I had waited on that other table."

"Why not?"

"Because I'm a nice guy," he declared, a noticeable twinkle in his eyes.

"Thanks, Jeremy." I set the money aside, then took my right foot out of the boot and propped both feet up in the chair closest to me. Jeremy sipped at his bottle, then glanced my way.

"You want one?" He pointed the neck of the bottle in my direction, like it was a compass.

"No thanks." I sat back in the chair, closed my eyes, and let my entire body relax.

"You don't drink, do you?" he wondered, before taking another swig.

"Not really." I felt my cheeks blush, giving me away. I would have been terrible at poker.

"Is that the truth?" Jeremy eyed me carefully, his ginger locks glowing beneath the lights.

"Honestly? I've never touched the stuff." I held his gaze, unashamed of my abstinence.

"Because you're not twenty-one yet, or what?" Jeremy leaned forward and dug his elbows into the table. If anyone else had asked, I would have felt cornered. But Jeremy wasn't the prying type. He just liked to talk.

"It's just not my thing," I affirmed. He nodded, not minding either way.

"That's cool," he said. "I respect your free will."

An enormous smile came over my face, because I had never heard such a respectful response. Most people thought I was a freak when I told them I didn't drink, never had, and never intended to. Regardless, I never caved, too solid to give in to the pressure. In their defense, most people just didn't understand the fact that alcohol was a toxic, poisonous liquid that destroyed the body, mind, and soul. But then again, most people hadn't known my father.

"So who was that guy tonight?" Jeremy asked.

"What guy?" I looked back at him, still lost in my daydream.

"You know which guy," he pressed. "The one sitting at the table you wanted me to wait on. I saw that terrified look in your eyes. What was that all about?"

"He's just an old friend, Jeremy. That's all."

"An old friend, huh? Yeah, I got a few of those, too," he quipped, sarcastic as ever.

"Hey!" I punched him in the bicep, though only in jest.

"Ow!" he grumbled. "That hurt!"

I giggled, gladly surrendering to the laughter.

"Did you have a rough week at school?" Jeremy swallowed more beer and waited.

"It was all right. Why?" I studied his evergreen eyes, so eager for information.

"It's just that, you don't laugh very often." His eyes sensed my inner sadness, my inner struggle, my inner longing. I shrugged my shoulders in acceptance and rested my arms on the chair.

My heart had been broken in two. How else was I expected to feel?

In an instant, Jeremy's face lit up, and he

jumped to his feet. "I know what you need." He waved a finger at me, the overzealous grin on his face sending nervous energy through my fingertips. "Stay right here. I'll be right back."

Jeremy left me alone in the dining room, as I heard him banging around in the kitchen. Taking a moment to rest my eyes, I lolled my head back and sighed aloud. For someone who liked being alone, it sure was nice to have someone to talk to.

When Jeremy came back, I opened my eyes and tensed at the sight of him. In his arms, Jeremy had managed to carry a bowl, two spoons, a half-gallon container of ice cream, and a mug filled to the brim with root beer. I pulled my feet out of the chair, making room for Jeremy, as he set everything down on the table.

"What are you doing?" I demanded, on the edge of giggling again.

"Don't tell me you've never had a root beer float before," he said with mock amusement.

I shook my head to the left and right, but Jeremy didn't say anything.

For the next couple of minutes, I looked on with wonder, as he plopped several spoonfuls of ice cream into the bowl, and then poured root beer on top. Sitting up straight, I watched the frothy dessert fizz and bubble, until Jeremy handed me a spoon.

"Try it," he nudged, like a candy maker in a chocolate factory.

Excited, I dipped my spoon into the floating

island of cream and bliss, then raised it to my lips. When the sweet confection entered my mouth, melting and cooling, I closed my eyes and let the sensation sink in. I had never tasted anything like it.

"Well?" Jeremy stood by the table, enjoying my obvious gratification.

"It's great, Jeremy," I announced. "Thank you."

"Well, have all you want. I should get going." He pointed to the digital watch around his wrist. "It's getting late." I reached for my boot, but Jeremy protested. "No, you stay. Don't feel like you have to leave, just because I am."

"You're sure it's okay?" I folded my fingers together, worried that I was intruding.

"Yes, Finley. I'm sure." Jeremy bent down, placed his hand on my shoulder, and then kissed my hair. "Just lock up when you're done, okay?"

I nodded, as he stepped back and headed towards the door.

"Why are you so sweet?" I asked, overwhelmed with his kindness and affection.

"Because I want to be." Jeremy held my gaze for a precious second, and I saw the adoration in his eyes. "Have a good time tonight, Finley." He crossed the threshold, letting the door swing shut behind him, and then he was gone.

Alone with my thoughts, I scooped another spoonful of ice cream into my bowl and kept my head down. Out of the corner of my eye, I noticed another spoon on the table, the one that Jeremy had brought. I picked up the spoon and frowned, unable to understand why Jeremy would grab a second spoon, and then not eat any himself. He hadn't touched the root beer float.

"I hope you saved some for me."

I whipped my head around and gasped at the sight of Cabel standing in the dining room.

Chapter 28

C abel?" I set the spoon down on the table and watched him stalk towards me. "What are you doing here? I thought you already left."

"Why did you send another waiter over to my table?" He pulled out the chair where I had rested my feet earlier and sat down.

"Um-"

"You didn't want to see me?" Cabel knitted his brows together, the hurt apparent in his piercing blue eyes. I leaned my shoulders back and sighed, letting my eyes dance across the table. We hadn't spoken in weeks, but it felt like ages since he had said my name.

"I thought that you and Pam were..." I searched for the word, my mind automatically blocking it out. "Together," I finally uttered.

"Oh," Cabel realized. His face took on a whole new shape, his eyes brighter, his cheeks trying to hide the undertone of a shy smile. He was relieved.

Returning to the root beer float, I picked my spoon up and skimmed the edge of the frothy, foamy concoction. Then I slipped a creamy spoonful into my mouth and focused on the fizzy coldness. Cabel's eyes remained on my face, as I carelessly ignored him.

"You haven't been by my office in weeks," he accused.

"I didn't know I was welcome," I fired back. My gaze lingered on the dessert bowl, while Cabel scoffed at my remark. "You're the one who told me to stop coming, Cabel. The reason why I don't go to your office anymore is because you told me not to."

Cabel clenched his fist and hunched over the table, biting his tongue. When I avoided him, he grasped my fingers in his hand, and I stilled. His touch had been taken away from me, right when I needed it most. Now that it had returned, my skin tingled with the same lingering excitement of a first kiss.

"I miss you," he whispered.

Jerking my fingers from his grasp, I pulled back and glowered at him. "Don't say things like that to me," I snapped. "You're only making it worse."

"But Finley-"

"Stop!" I reached down and strapped my foot into the boot, in case I should need to escape sometime in the near future. "Just stop it!"

Slinging my hair back, I sat up in the chair and scoffed, tired of his effect on my emotions. When I held my jaw taut and stared, Cabel grabbed the extra spoon that Jeremy had left behind, and then eyed my root beer float. Before the mouth of his spoon could meet the creamy dessert, I stood up, snatched the bowl off the table, and marched through the dining room until I reached the kitchen.

I tossed the bowl in the sink, relishing the loud crash that sounded as a result. Cabel followed me into the kitchen, hot on my heels, but I could care less. He had tormented me enough by boxing up his affection and locking it away. I would never lose myself in his arms again.

"Finley," Cabel groaned, but I kept my back to him, splashing water over the few dishes that were left in the sink. "Look, I know you're upset, all right? But I'm sorry."

He touched the back of my shoulders, putting me on edge. So I moved towards the island, at the center of the kitchen, and began wiping the already spotless surface down with a dish cloth.

"Finley," Cabel whined. "Come on. Talk to me."

I stopped circling the cloth over the counter and glanced back at him. The look in his eyes told me everything I needed to know.

"You were right," I confessed. "This could never work."

"No," he denied, taking a step forward. "Finley, I was wrong. I'm sorry. I never should have said those things to you in my office that day."

Feeling my heart swell with elation, I turned

back to the kitchen island and resumed my cleaning. After everything Cabel had said to me, I didn't want to refashion a bond with him that would most definitely be broken. We just needed to accept what was.

Cabel was a professor, and I was his student.

Truthfully, there was nothing more to say.

"Finley," he nagged, grating on my nerves. No matter how fast I walked around the island, Cabel was still right behind me. "Finley!"

"What?" I spun around to face him, fear and anger and passion pouring from my soul.

Fear for the possibility of losing Cabel for good; anger for him shutting me out of his life so coldly; and passion for the desirous love that he had refused to let me have, when I had willingly offered my own.

"I want to be with you," he said, his voice husky, deep, and heart-rattling. The thought of such a reality was too painful to bear, because it couldn't be real or sustainable. It would only lead to another line of cracks in my broken heart.

"I don't want to have this conversation with you, Cabel."

"I'll wait for you," he promised.

My heart began to pound at a frantic rhythm, forcing the sound of loud, pulsing blood in my ears. I pressed my palms into the counter and held on for dear life. When I turned my face towards Cabel, he tucked a dark strand of hair behind my ear and exhaled through his nose.

"What did you say?" I breathed.

"I'll wait for you, Finley," Cabel repeated. "However long it takes, and we can figure something out until you graduate." He brushed his knuckles over my cheek, and I thought I might faint.

"No," I demanded, retreating to the opposite side of the island. "I don't want to do that."

"Why?" Cabel asked, keeping his distance.

"We can't be together, Cabel," I growled, mad that he was making me spell it out for him. "It's never going to work." And then, I felt Monty's words haunting me, as they left my mouth. "We're not right for each other."

"Yeah, we are, Finley," Cabel disagreed. He came close enough to touch me, and I put my hand up in protest. Tears were already pooling in my eyes, blurring my vision.

"Please, Cabel," I sobbed. "Just go."

"All right." He cocked his head to the side, like he was taking on a challenge. "I'll go, but I'm going to kiss you first. And if you still want me to leave then, I'll never bother you again."

"Cabel, don't," I begged, holding my hands in the air to keep him at bay. But that only made the man in him act faster.

Ignoring my request, Cabel took my face in his hands and clamped his mouth to mine. Tears ran down my cheeks, as he tore my lips apart, his sweet breath flowing in. When I sighed, Cabel dug his fingers into my hair and pulled my face even closer to his, consuming me, tasting me, cherishing me.

Our last kiss felt every bit as good as the first. Only, the first had been more pleasure than pain. The last practically turned me into a masochist, because I craved that sweet torture above all else.

"I'm in love with you," I cried against his mouth, unable to restrain myself. Cabel pulled me into his chest, as I bent my arms and sandwiched them between our torsos.

"I know," he coaxed, running his hand over my hair. "Because I'm in love with you, too."

Cabel held me close, clutching my body against his chest.

"You said things have to go back to the way they were," I sniffled. "Why won't you let them?" I smelled the cologne on his neck, and knew what I had to do. "You have to go, Cabel."

My heart shattered into a million pieces, as I pulled out of his warm, affectionate embrace. Drying my eyes, I returned to the sink and splashed cool water on my face. When Cabel called my name, I looked back over my shoulder at him.

"I love you, Finley," he confessed. "I'll always love you. And I'm waiting, whether you want me to or not."

Cabel pushed through the swinging door and left me alone in the kitchen, exactly as I had asked him to do.

* * *

At the end of finals week, I saw Cabel for the last time in his office. Holding back my tears, I sat down at the chair in front of his desk and handed him the textbook that I had been using all semester. The one that he had let me borrow.

"I don't want it anymore," I softly muttered.

"Finley, please keep it," Cabel said. "That book is yours. If you don't want it, at least take it to the bookstore and sell it."

I reached into my bag and pulled out a shiny red apple. "For old time's sake," I offered.

With all the emotional strength I could muster, I rose to my feet, left the apple on his desk, and headed towards the doorway. I should have heard Cabel calling after me, but my mind was so focused on fleeing, that I hardly noticed the sound of his voice. Instead, I placed my hand on the doorknob and swallowed.

"Goodbye, Mr. Jones."

I didn't look back.

Part III

The Old Friend

TWO YEARS LATER...

Chapter 29

A flock of graduation caps soared into the air, then came crashing down among hundreds of former seniors. I looked around the auditorium, watching parents, grandparents, brothers, and sisters find their loved ones in the crowd, congratulating the happy graduate with hugs and kisses. But there was no one waiting for me.

Feeling glum, I locked myself in a bathroom stall and let the tears flow until I tasted warm salt. I unzipped the black gown that I had been required to wear over my knee-length dress: a simple, black garment, with ruffles of creamy white satin beneath the collar. Then I took my graduation cap off, ripped the tassel from the round button at the center of the fabric, and tossed it onto the dirty tile floor.

All I had ever wanted was a family. Instead, I had been raised in the homes of disinterested strangers, who would have rather not had me around. All these years later, I couldn't think of the first foster parent who would care to know that I had just graduated from college.

So, what did it matter if I had a diploma? There was no point in celebrating my academic achievements, because I had no one to share them with.

My mother was dead, and my father might as well have been, with his time on death row quickly running out. No one loved me, but maybe that was my fault. I had been the one to live as a recluse for most of my life, never seeking out friendships, never being the first one to start a conversation, never attempting to shed my introverted skin.

I was distrusting by nature, rarely giving a person the benefit of the doubt. Trust no one. That had become my new mantra in recent years. There was no purpose in wearing your heart on your sleeve, because someone would just steal the fabric and burn it.

After drying my eyes and splashing water on my face in the sink, I felt brave enough to walk back into the auditorium. But by the time I finally did, everyone was gone. So, I headed for the exit sign and left the building, anxious to be far away from my pain, my tears, my past.

A few families were still outside, taking pictures in front of the elaborate, classically-styled auditorium. I had never been a terribly envious person, but in that moment, I envied every college graduate who had a family, who had a mother that was still alive, who had a father that hadn't killed her. Why did they get to have one when I didn't?

With my head down, I drug my feet across the

pavement and trudged towards the parking lot. I knew that I wouldn't be able to sleep tonight, but not for the reasons that every other college graduate had. Since I didn't have a party to go to, I settled on the idea of watching a romantic tearjerker on the couch, with a tub of microwaved popcorn in my lap.

Just when I thought my melancholia had gotten the best of me, I saw something out of the corner of my eye and looked up. Cabel stood by a cool stone fountain that sat between the auditorium and parking lot, his blonde hair glowing beneath the street lamps. He was dressed in a suit and tie, carrying a dozen red roses, and nervously pacing back and forth.

An unexpected smile came across my face, as I shook my head. Walking over, I took a handful of long, careful strides, until I reached the fountain. Any other time, my heart would have been beating so violently inside of my chest that I could hardly breathe. But tonight, I felt calm for a change. When Cabel had yet to notice me, I cleared my throat, and he turned around.

"Mr. Jones," I addressed. "What are you doing here?"

As Cabel straightened his posture, I surveyed his ageless appearance. It had been two years, but I hardly saw any indication in his youthful face that the time had passed. His golden blonde locks were cut just the same, short and straight, while his icy blue eyes looked just as I had remembered them, like an arctic, frozen glacier drifting in the sea.

"I came to see you graduate," Cabel said.

He held the roses out for me to take, and then grinned when I accepted them. Delighted, I lowered my face over the soft red petals and inhaled. They smelled like heaven.

"How did you know I was graduating tonight?" I tucked the bouquet beneath my arm, along with my graduation cap and gown, then returned my focus to Cabel.

"I have my sources," he vaguely replied, curving his mouth into a tasteful smirk.

For a brief moment, I recalled the sound of someone whistling when I had walked across the stage to receive my diploma. It must have been Cabel.

"But I graduated a year early," I noted. "How did you know about that?"

Even now, I could decipher Cabel's attitude in the moonlight. He was disappointed, because I had yet to acknowledge the sudden reality of our situation. I wasn't a student anymore.

"Why did you?" he asked.

To be free of you, I thought. *To be free of those nights in the forest.*

The pain crept back into my veins, pulsing in my ears, as I recollected my broken heart. The heart that he had broken, the heart that I had given him, the heart that I didn't want back.

"Why did you come, Cabel?" I snapped. "I

didn't ask you to be here."

Honestly, I was embarrassed. I didn't want Cabel to see me here with no family and no friends. It was humiliating, and he hadn't been invited.

"I wanted to be here for you, Finley," he crooned.

But Cabel's words only upset me further. He had taken pity on me, simply because I had no one else. Cabel had come tonight for one reason. He felt sorry for me.

"Like you have been for the past two years," I countered.

Before Cabel could respond, I shoved the roses into his chest and stormed off. I had endured enough sleepless nights, thinking about Cabel and those precious, fleeting moments we had shared, all the while wondering why fate had dealt me such a cruel hand of cards. Tonight was not going to be one of them.

"Finley, wait!" Cabel called, coming after me. When I kept walking, he grabbed my arm and pulled me back. "I'm sorry. Okay? I'm sorry for abandoning you and pushing you away. But I had no choice. Can't you see that?" I tried to break free from his grasp, but Cabel braced my shoulders with his hands. "Finley, listen to me," he begged. "Please."

"Let me go," I growled. I felt his breath against my mouth, and it brought so many old, unhealed wounds to the surface. If I gazed into those icy blue eyes, I knew that I would never miss seeing them again.

"I meant what I said that night at the restaurant," Cabel murmured. "I love you, Finley. And I've waited for you, just like I told you I would." I felt his eyes on my face, but couldn't look at him. "I wanted to make things work back then," he confessed. "But I let you go, because I thought that was what you wanted me to do." Cabel searched my face and waited, patient as ever.

"Cabel," I sobbed, feeling my insides turn soft, as they melted like warm chocolate.

"Just tell me, Finley." He turned my chin up with his thumb and finger, forcing me to acknowledge his pleading demands. The subtle touch crept across every inch of my skin, spiraling outward into a web of burning desire. "Do you love me or not?"

Cabel looked so young, so innocent, bearing his soul to me by the cool mist of the fountain. I lowered my eyelashes, and then glanced up at him from beneath them. "Cabel," I whimpered.

"Just answer the question," he ordered, mesmerizing me with his frosty blue stare.

"Please," I cried. "Just let me go." Tears streamed down my cheeks, pouring out in heavy waves. My vision grew blurry, but all I felt was tired. My heart couldn't endure another break.

"No!" he refused. "I will never let you go."

Before I could protest, Cabel leaned in and

molded his mouth to mine, delicately braiding his fingers through my hair. I let out a staggering sigh, as my breathing grew unsteady, but Cabel silenced me with the tingling, electric touch of his lips. Relying on impulse alone, I wrapped my arms around his neck and sank into the length of his body, while Cabel pulled me against him, planting a firm grip at the small of my back.

I hadn't been kissed in so long that Cabel's lips tasted like honey -- sweet, golden, and pure. When he clasped my bottom lip between his teeth, I moaned at the pleasurable agony, because I hadn't felt the rush of heat beneath my skin in years. I surrendered my mouth to his warm, sensual ways, and then dug my fingernails into the back of his neck when there was no other way to handle the sensation.

Shivers traveled throughout my body, all the way to the tips of my toes, as every nerve ending came alive with fire. I tugged at the lapels of Cabel's jacket and struggled to keep my balance, willing to forego breathing if that would keep his lips on mine. When his strong hands began kneading the flesh of my back through my dress, I gasped at the power of his touch.

Cabel wanted me just as badly as I wanted him.

"I've lived without you for two years, Finley," he panted, holding his mouth above mine. I felt the buckle of his belt against my stomach, but didn't mind. "Please don't make me do it anymore."

His knuckles traced patterns over my face, as he lovingly gazed into my eyes. I took my time catching my breath, searching the depths of his light, sparkling eyes, so clear blue that they looked like crystals. My body throbbed with desire, and I worried that he could feel my thumping pulse, when his fingertips lingered at the junction of my neck and shoulder.

For so long, I had convinced myself that I had done something wrong, that I had overstepped a boundary, that I had been the only one to make a mistake. But it wasn't true.

I had picked the apple, but Cabel had taken the first bite.

"Let me take you out to dinner," he enticed, "to celebrate."

Steadying myself, I looked into his eyes and pressed my lips together. Despite the years of distance between us, I felt just as connected to Cabel as I had ever been, just as heated, just as passionate. A smoldering burn had returned to that hollow, empty place inside of me, and Cabel had been the one to put it there.

"Every restaurant's probably already booked up," I breathed, my voice nearly a whisper.

Cabel smiled, and then knelt down to gather the bouquet of roses, as well as my cap and gown. I blushed at the realization that I had tossed my belongings to the ground, too wrapped up in his arms and affection to notice otherwise. He handed me the roses, stuck my graduation cap beneath his arm, and then draped my gown over his shoulder.

"It's all right," he assured me. "I think I know a place."

Cabel's eyes glazed over my figure, as the reality of his intentions settled in. Neither of us was forbidden to each other anymore, which meant that I could have every inch of Cabel that I desired. Only, I wasn't the same girl that he had known in the forest. I had changed.

Losing Cabel had been the cause of that, but I blamed myself for turning into a colder, darker, harder version of my former self. There was no doubt in my mind that I was my father's daughter, especially when my spirit began to freeze in places that I didn't know could survive without warmth. I had felt so alone and so miserable and so wretched. Utterly hopeless, I had thought that there was nothing left for me... until now.

Cabel slipped his arm around my waist and led me towards the parking lot, while I relished his tight embrace. After all this time, paradise loomed before me in the walking image of Cabel Jones. The only man I had ever loved. And despite the jagged, frozen pieces of my broken heart that wanted nothing more desperately than to crack, I knew that I had to try.

Chapter 30

With my hands on the steering wheel, I looked through my car window and marveled at the scattered gathering of twinkling white stars up above. Cabel drove his car in front of mine, while I followed closely behind, intrigued by the lonely two-lane highway he was leading me down. My heart was pounding, flooding warm blood through my veins at the excitement.

Cabel turned onto a narrow canopy road and coasted along the pavement for no more than a mile, before signaling to the left. Reeling, I glanced to the rearview mirror, and then watched him pull into a steep, gravel-covered driveway that was surrounded by forest on either side. With a deep sigh, I shifted into a lower gear, pressed my foot on the gas pedal, and trailed Cabel's car up the hill.

Towering trees stood mighty and robust, dominating the tract of land before us. A wave of nostalgia swept through me, as images of our time in the cabin came back to haunt me. In the past two years, I had yet to forget the way Cabel's face had looked, covered in soot from the fire. If only that had been the most disturbing memory of those days in the forest.

At the top of the incline, Cabel followed the curve of the driveway, until a quiet, secluded two-story house appeared before us. My eyes widened at the perfect brick structure, complete with wide windows, red gables, and a wooden swing on the front porch. I could already imagine smoke billowing out from the chimney, when winter came, and a playful, frolicking hound dog wagging his tail in the front yard. I wondered if Cabel was picturing the same.

After parking my car beside Cabel's, I stepped out and gazed up at the house. I heard the sound of leaves crunching beneath Cabel's shoes, as he approached, a placid look on his face.

"I thought you had an apartment in town," I began, remembering something he had once said.

"I did." Cabel shifted on his feet, then shoved his hands in his pockets. My arms dangled over my car door, while I studied Cabel in the soft moonlight. "I guess I just got tired of the city."

"So you decided to move out here," I paused, "to the middle of nowhere?"

Cabel chuckled, his dark laughter sending heat along the back of my neck. When he turned towards me, I felt my will power beginning to wither beneath those husky blue eyes. Before I knew it, there was nothing more than the car door standing between us.

"It's quiet out here," he noted.

"Hmm," I lilted, paralyzed by his presence.

Cabel took my hand in his, and then shut the car door, leading me towards the front porch. My heels clicked against the wooden boards, as Cabel rifled for keys in his pocket. I studied the empty swing by the door and wondered what it would be like to lay there in Cabel's lap.

"Ready?" Cabel raised his eyebrows in devilish delight.

"Yeah," I whispered, nodding and blushing, all at the same time.

Opening the door, Cabel extended his hand and motioned for me to step inside. I crossed the threshold with my arms over my chest, then leaned my head back to observe the spacious foyer, high ceilings, and hardwood floors. A large staircase stood just past the entrance, with a series of wide, carpet-covered steps that led to the second floor.

"Go ahead," Cabel welcomed. "Have a look around." He locked the front door, turned to the right, and entered a corridor that led to places I had yet to see. I missed him already.

Letting my eyes flicker across the foyer, I placed my hands on my hips and sighed. I had yet to understand why Cabel had moved to the wilderness, where he would have no neighbors, no streetlights, and no noise. The thought unsettled me, because I had been surviving on the late night disturbances of restless co-eds for years at my apartment complex, living vicariously through the sounds of others. Then again, now that Cabel had brought me here, we were finally alone.

While I sorted through my thoughts, a pair of French doors caught my eye in the foyer. Curious, I stepped to the left side of the room and placed my arms behind my back, nestling my elbow in my hand. As I approached the glass, Cabel's office came into view, so I twisted the door handle and let myself inside.

Perfectly polished bookshelves lined the walls, not unlike the layout of Cabel's office at school. I was happy to see that his organizational skills had not diminished in recent years, as every book appeared to be in alphabetical order from where I was standing. A certain spine caught the corner of my eye, so I walked between the leather couch against the wall and the desk by the door, anxious to pull the book from its place on the shelf.

When I did, a sense of familiarity washed over me, because I was holding the hardbound textbook that Cabel had used to teach clinical psychology, during the semester that I had first known him as my professor. Smiling, I opened the first page and found an inscription on the inside of the front cover.

For Miss Finley O'Connell

I stared at those words for a long time, hardly able to believe that Cabel had kept the book, after everything that had happened between us. Not wanting to relive old memories, I shut the hardback and returned it to the bookshelf where I had found it. Then I left Cabel's office, pulled the French doors shut behind me, and headed upstairs.

When I reached the top of the staircase, I dropped my hand from the banister and wandered down a long corridor, peeking my head through the entryway to each room. In total, I counted four bedrooms, three bathrooms, a laundry room, and a sizable bonus room that Cabel had converted into an area purely designated for entertainment. Once I reached the other end of the hallway, I found a room in the corner that I had overlooked, simply because the door was closed. Falling prey to my own curiosity, I looked back over my shoulder, and then entered the last room.

As I opened the door, my eyes searched the lofty master bedroom and widened with intrigue. Sauntering over the soft carpet, I admired the regal four-poster bed that sat against the wall, blanketed in cool, white sheets. Fine furniture filled the rest of the room, a chest of drawers to the left side of the bed, a dresser with a mirror attached to the right. Cabel's walk-in closet had enough space to accommodate the clothing and accessories of five people, while the private bathroom appeared just as capacious with open tile floors, a tub and shower, and double sinks.

Returning to the four-poster bed, I climbed onto the mattress and took a seat. Only one question came to mind, as I flattened my hand against the white linen comforter.

What was Cabel doing in this big house all by himself?

"What do you think?"

I looked up, startled by the sudden timbre of Cabel's voice. When he walked into the bedroom and stalked closer, I licked my lips, before pressing them together in anticipation.

"It's a really nice house, Cabel," I commented. "When did you move in?"

"About six months ago," he murmured, no longer wearing his jacket or tie.

"Someone sold you the place?" I inquired.

"No." Cabel frowned. "I had the house built."

"Really?" I knitted my eyebrows together, not expecting that response.

"Yeah," he breathed. "I bought the land first, as an investment, but I guess it grew on me."

Casting my eyes down, I twisted my fingers together and watched the way it made my knuckles bend. Cabel placed one hand over my fists and the other against the side of my face, seamlessly easing my restless state of mind. Everything about tonight felt like a dream, because Cabel had come back, and he still wanted me.

"Let's go downstairs," he suggested. "I want to show you the rest of the house."

On the first floor, Cabel gave me a tour of every place that I had yet to see, pulling me from the dining room to the living room to the kitchen. Eventually, I found myself on the back deck, gazing out at the moonlit forest before us. It felt like many moons had passed since graduation.

By the time we sat down to eat dinner, I couldn't think about anything other than the fact that I was starving. Cabel placed two plates with steak, boiled potatoes, and string beans on the dining room table, as I spread my napkin out in my lap. If his new house, good manners, and tasteful cooking weren't enough, Cabel had left my roses soaking in a vase full of fresh water on the kitchen counter. Because, apparently, Cabel had thought of everything.

"I didn't know you liked to cook," I started.

Cabel sat down across from me, while I brushed my thumb along the metal tines of my fork. When Cabel took a sip of water from his glass, I worried that he was ignoring me. But then his eyes returned to mine, and I felt my skin flush at the way those blue gems drifted down my face.

"I don't." Cabel cut into his steak, slicing tiny chunks, as I gathered my utensils.

"You didn't have to do all of this," I replied, noticing the change in his voice.

"I wanted to," Cabel asserted, his eyes on me.

My breathing hitched, as he stabbed a piece of meat with his fork, slid the utensil into his mouth, and then scraped his white teeth against the metal prongs on their way out. His behavior clouded my thoughts, so I let my mind wander, in the process of devouring every string bean on my plate. By the time I started on my steak and potatoes, I couldn't bear the silence.

"Why did you bring me here, Cabel?" I asked. He set his fork down, swallowed, and then wiped his mouth with the napkin in his lap. "What is all of this about?"

"Finley," Cabel scolded, shaking his head. "I've made it very clear how I feel about you."

"I know." My eyes descended, as I watched my fingers fold over the napkin across my thighs.

"I'm sorry about the past couple of years," he apologized. "But you have to understand." Cabel rested his hand over his chest, his long masculine fingers splayed out. "I'm a professor, and you were my student. I couldn't touch you then."

"But now that you can, you want to," I accused, levelling my eyes at him.

Cabel closed his eyes, gritting his teeth, as his nostrils flared. Despite every good intention, Cabel could not turn back the clock and mold me into the girl he once knew. I was different now, and afraid that I had changed too indelibly, that too much time had passed between us, that whatever chance we had of being together was long gone.

"I should go," I muttered. "I don't even know what I'm doing here."

"Wait." Cabel grabbed my hand and pinned it to the table.

I took a gasp of air and exhaled, "Cabel."

"Finley, please don't go," he pleaded.

I felt the tears brewing, as that hard knot formed in my throat. Cabel wrapped his other hand around my wrist and willed me to meet the icy blue stillness in his eyes. When I did, a strange, numbing sensation settled in the pit of my stomach. I couldn't breathe.

"What do I have to do to make you stay?"

"You want me to stay?"

"Yes," he hissed, demanding, yet vulnerable.

"Why?" I tilted my head to the side and stared.

"Because you're the best thing that's ever happened to me."

Biting my tongue, I kept my head down and let tears blur my vision. When I offered no other reaction, Cabel pushed his chair back, stood up, and knelt down on the floor in front of me.

"Finley, those few nights in the forest meant everything to me," he urged, turning my face up in his hands. Cabel stroked the length of my jawline, his thumbs and fingers dancing across the surface of my skin. My heart was thrumming, pulsing, melting. I had never felt like this before.

"What happens now?" I prompted, gazing down at him from underneath my lashes.

"Everything."

Chapter 31

After dinner, Cabel left me alone in the dining room, only to return with a square package that was covered in silver wrapping paper. I sat up in my chair, eyeing the item curiously, as he set it down on the table in front of me. When I grinned like a child, Cabel's eyes lit up.

"It's not much, but I hope you like it." Cabel returned to his seat and smiled. I picked the package up and shook it in my hand, unable to guess the mystery item.

"What is it?" I looked at Cabel, adoring the way he was looking at me.

"Your graduation present," he answered. "Go on. Open it."

Captivated, I slipped my fingernail beneath a strip of tape and tore the wrapping paper back. My eyes widened with surprise, then happiness, then tears of joy. Cabel had given me *I Love Lucy: The Complete Series* - every episode of my beloved TV show on DVD in one box set. If my mother had been alive, she would have told me that Cabel was a keeper, right then and there.

"I'm sorry," Cabel said, noticing the tears in

my eyes. "I didn't mean to make you upset."

"No," I sobbed. "I love it, Cabel." A thousand different emotions raced through me.

Before Cabel could say anything, I rose from my seat and buried my face in his chest. He wrapped me in his arms, holding me close, while I inhaled the familiar scent of his cologne.

"I've missed you," I confessed.

Cabel's hands traveled the length of my back, as he said, "I've missed you, too."

For the longest time, I never thought I'd see him again. I didn't want to see him again. I had thought Cabel Jones was no more than a pipe dream, meant to torment me forever, meant to tease me with the prospect of what I could never have. Now, I realized how wrong I had been.

"Do you want to go upstairs?" Cabel whispered in my ear.

Breathless, I pulled my head back, met Cabel's sultry gaze, and nodded.

For the next four hours, Cabel and I watched back-to-back episodes of *I Love Lucy* in the bonus room upstairs. With my legs sprawled out on the couch, I enjoyed every minute of Lucy's hilarious antics in a state of complete relaxation. I hadn't felt that calm in a while.

As the night wore on, Cabel kept his arm wrapped tightly around my waist, clutching me to his side. I had the feeling that he wasn't going to let me out of his grasp, but I liked the fact that he was clinging to me. After two years alone, I desperately wanted someone to hold on to.

Eventually, the long day caught up with me, as the lively characters on the TV screen became blurry and distorted. I hadn't slept well in ages, maybe ever, but tonight was different. Cabel Jones had come back into my life, sheltering me with pure warmth, as I felt the frozen pieces of my heart beginning to thaw and mend. I never wanted to be cold again.

Feeling safe, I rested my head on Cabel's shoulder and closed my eyes.

* * *

My eyelashes fluttered as I stirred awake, plagued by the memory of a heart-wrenching nightmare. In recent months, the dreams had only gotten worse, and I began to worry that they would never stop, never go away, never let me rest in peace.

I sat up in Cabel's four-poster bed and looked around the room, surprised by how different things looked in the daylight. Cabel slept soundlessly beside me, his face soft and peaceful, his golden, muscular back exposed, creating a striking contrast against the white sheets. Carefully peeling the covers back, I glanced down at the oversized t-shirt I was wearing, whose fabric bore the word *CORNELL*. My mouth fell open, as I realized what Cabel had done.

"I didn't think you'd be comfortable sleeping in that dress," he murmured.

Pulsing hot blood rushed to my cheeks. "You took my clothes off?"

Cabel smirked. "It's not like I haven't done it before."

Narrowing my eyes, I playfully slapped Cabel on the arm, but he seemed to like it. Before I could withdraw my hand, he clamped down on my wrist and pulled me under the covers with him. The side of my face brushed against the pillow, as Cabel flattened his palm against my back.

"I'm glad you stayed." His eyes pleasantly dilated, the ice blue waning around those dark pupils, thickening with blackness. I lay beside him in the bed, adoring the way his arm felt around my body. When he stroked his fingers through my long, dark tresses, I sighed.

"I am too." A sense of peace drifted through me, calming my spirit. For the moment, my loud, rambling thoughts had ceased, and my mind was quiet. "So, what happened last night?"

"Nothing," Cabel said, burying his head in the pillow. "You fell asleep."

I lowered my gaze, averted my eyes, and then lost my peaceful state of mind altogether. Even Cabel couldn't permanently remove the damage from my subconscious, like scar tissue that wouldn't stop forming, expanding, growing. What would it take to heal these wounds?

"Finley, who's been chasing you in your dreams?" Cabel tilted my chin up, and then brushed his thumb along the length of my jawbone. "You didn't sleep well last night," he added.

I shook my head and kept my eyes down, ignoring the concerned look on his face.

"Just memories," I mumbled, making light of the violent nightmares.

"About your father?" he assumed, his eyes filled with awareness.

"Yes." I put my head on his shoulder and leaned into the weight of his body.

"Finley," Cabel spoke, his breath on my neck. "He doesn't have much time left."

Freezing, I pulled out of his embrace and stared. "How do you know about that?"

Cabel lowered his lashes, exhaled through his nostrils, and then pushed the covers back. I looked on in confusion, as he got out of the bed and walked over to his dresser. He opened the bottom drawer with his back to me, then returned to the bed with two tickets in his hand.

Plane tickets.

"I think you should go see him," Cabel suggested, though the prospect didn't sound optional.

"Well," I swallowed, defensive, "I don't think it's any of your business."

"Finley," Cabel groaned, reaching for my hand. "If you don't do it now, you'll regret it later." I pulled my knees into my chest and pressed my back into the headboard, nervous and weary. "You have no idea how many things I've wanted to say to my parents. And now I can't anymore."

"You just don't understand." I slid off the mattress, walked around the foot of the bed, and began pacing back and forth. "The thought of having to look at him," I cried, my voice cracking. "After what he did..." I trailed off, running my hands over my face with worry.

"By the end of the week, it won't matter how you felt right now," Cabel claimed.

"Cabel, I-"

"Listen to me," he interrupted, peeling my hands from my face. I looked away and grumbled, ready to crawl back under the covers and hide. "I'm saying this because I love you." Cabel lifted my face in his hands, compelling me to gaze into his eyes. "You need to see your father."

"Why?" I countered.

"Because I'm not the only man in your life."

Plagued by my inner struggle, I fought the urge to scream. Cabel didn't know how right he was, or how badly I wished he had been wrong. Over a decade had passed since I had last seen my father, but it felt like no more than a day. No matter how many years went by, I had never been able to escape the feeling that he wasn't far away, our final encounter still on the surface of my mind. A memory that wouldn't dissipate. I had to face him again, only this time, I wasn't alone.

"Okay," I consented. "I'll go."

Cabel kissed my forehead, and then hugged me close, pressing his body against mine. I could already feel my hands beginning to tremble, the overwhelming anxiety seeping through my skin.

"Everything's going to be all right," he promised. "I won't make you go in there alone."

"Thank you," I exhaled in relief. Cabel patted my cheek, and then withdrew his hand.

"Get dressed. If we're going to go, we need to leave soon."

I crossed my arms over my chest, already starting to feel cold. Cabel walked into the bathroom and turned the shower on, while I stood at the foot of the bed, still wearing his t-shirt. My temples started to throb, my head aching, my bones stiff and rigid. I didn't want to do this, but I had to.

Cabel was right; he wasn't the only man in my life. But soon, he would be.

Chapter 32

The plane ride didn't last as long as I had hoped. Cabel squeezed my hand, while we touched down in my hometown. The place I swore I would never return. The place I no longer belonged. The place I would never name.

Looking out the window, I felt my eyes drifting across the familiar terrain, scanning and searching for all the things that had changed in my absence. My mother would never get to see this place and watch it age, watch it slowly evolve over time, until it eventually turned into something else. Something green and fresh. Something new. Something neither of us would have ever recognized.

"Are you ready to go?" Cabel kept his eyes on me, but I could barely speak.

"Yes," I breathed, my voice strained and unfamiliar. As much as this place was to me now. This place that I had once called home.

Feeling the weight of a thousand monkeys on my back, I stood behind Cabel at the airport desk designated for car rentals and leaned my head on his shoulder. Cabel wrapped his arm around my waist and pulled me into his side. I knew in my heart that I never would have come, if he hadn't been with me.

"Will that be all for you and your girlfriend today, Mr. Jones?" the rental agent asked. He had brown hair and a cute smile. I liked the way he called me Cabel's girlfriend. It sounded nice.

"Yes, thank you," Cabel answered. He lowered his face to mine and grinned, rubbing his hand over my back. When I turned pink in the cheeks, Cabel pulled his lips into a teasing smirk and chuckled. He hadn't corrected the rental agent, and I was surprised by how good that felt. After all of these lonely days apart, we were finally able to be together.

On the ride through town, I twisted my fingers in my lap, echoing the bundle of knots that had formed in the pit of my stomach. Cabel drove in silence. No radio. No conversation. No white noise to distract my frantic thoughts. I didn't know if I could do this, but that hardly mattered now.

"Are you okay?" Cabel finally spoke up, inadvertently reading my mind.

But my thoughts were elsewhere.

How could I bear to look into his dark brown eyes? My eyes? The eyes that he had given me. How I longed to have my mother's bright blue eyes, more like Cabel's than not. I wanted to belong wholly to my mother, be only her child, only her daughter. I didn't want any part of him. I wanted nothing of the man who had taken my mother from me.

"Finley?"

"What?" I snapped.

"Are you okay?" Cabel repeated, frustrated that I hadn't answered him the first time.

"I'm fine," I lied.

I was already on edge enough.

There was no need for both of us to be.

"Actually, I was wondering if we could stop by my mother's grave on the way." I looked out the window and imagined the silhouette of her face on the other side. She had been beautiful.

"Okay," Cabel agreed. "Just tell me how to get there."

* * *

When Cabel and I arrived at the cemetery, that familiar strain of terror rippled through me. The last time I had been here, a preacher had said some nice words, a crowd of loved ones had shed some tears, and my mother had been lowered beneath the earth in a pine box. Back then, all I had wanted to do was run, but my legs had lacked the strength.

Cabel placed his hand on my thigh, as I stiffened at the touch. "Are you ready?"

Voiceless, I nodded at the window, unable to look at anything other than the plot of land where they had buried her. Cabel got out of the car, and then walked around to open my door. I let him help me out, needing every bit of support that he was willing to offer. I didn't know how I was going to get through the day without perishing.

My mother's headstone had been neglected in recent years, the granite weathered and worn. I traced my finger over the etched lettering of her name, then pressed my thumb against her years of birth and death, absorbing the rough texture through my skin. A single white rose was all that I had brought her, so I gently laid it across the crest of the headstone and wept.

Cabel stood behind me, wrapping his arms around my stomach, as he leaned his head over my shoulder. I squeezed my eyes shut and let the tears leak out, feeling the warmth of Cabel's chest against my back. When I clutched Cabel's forearms and held them around me, the weight of the world didn't seem to be crashing down on my shoulders. But then I remembered the reason why we had come here, and all I could think about was Daddy.

* * *

The prison gates awaited me, those spiraling metal wires atop the length of the fence. My entire focus centered on the terribly rapid beating of my heart, painfully throbbing, though I tried to ignore it. Within minutes, the knots in my stomach had developed into hard rocks of discomfort, and I knew that I was going to vomit. Hyperventilating, I waved my hands in front of my face and fell into a heated panic in the passenger's seat.

"I can't do this," I confessed, utterly terrified.

"Finley," Cabel coaxed.

"I can't do it, and you're not going to make me!"

Cabel pulled onto the shoulder of the road and jerked the keys out of the ignition, the entrance to the prison looming before us. I rocked my head back and forth, then tucked it between my knees when the world began to spin around me. Everything was a blur of black and red.

"I can't see him. I just can't, Cabel! Don't you understand?" I cried, shaking and sobbing inconsolably. Bile settled at the base of my throat, ready to rise. I couldn't bear the taste.

"Don't you want to be free of him?" Cabel reasoned, trying to convince me. He tossed the keys in his lap and pointed at the prison. "Don't you want to be free of this?"

"I'll never be free of him," I slurred through my tears.

"If you don't do this now, you never will," Cabel demanded, cutting straight to the bone.

"I. Don't. Want. To. Do. This." I could barely speak in single syllables.

"What would your mother say?" he badgered. "What would she tell you to do?"

"Don't talk about my mother," I admonished. "You never knew her."

Cabel stopped talking, while I reveled in the silence. Here I was, so close to confronting my father and finally receiving the closure that I had always wanted, and I couldn't follow through. I couldn't finish what I had started. Every time I peered out the window, it felt like I couldn't breathe, like something was weighing on my chest, constricting my lungs, forcing the air elsewhere.

"I haven't seen him since I was ten," I revealed. "He may not even recognize me."

Cabel scoffed at my remark. "He'll recognize you, Finley."

I wildly shook my head from side to side, unable to stand the pressure, the pain, the past.

"You won't be going in there alone," Cabel reminded me.

I inhaled through my nose, and then breathed out a long sigh.

Somehow, Cabel persuaded me to stay, so I did.

Chapter 33

Inside the prison walls, I shivered in place, despite the spreading warmth throughout my body. Cabel draped his arm around my shoulders, in an attempt to calm my nerves, but it was no use. If I didn't have a heart attack, my lungs were going to burst into flames and then collapse.

One of the many prison guards approached, his face rigid and reserved. I curled my arms around Cabel, snuggling into him for support, heat, and a place to hide. I wasn't ready yet.

"You can go in and see him now," the guard said.

Cabel craned his neck to look down at me. "Are you ready?"

"Are you still coming with me?" I checked.

"Of course," he assured me, caressing my neck.

"No," the guard refused, "only her."

My eyes widened in panic, as I took a wobbly pair of steps backward, colliding with the wall. Cabel clutched my elbow and helped me regain my balance, but the dreaded terror remained.

"Cabel," I helplessly whimpered, "please don't

make me go in there alone."

"I'm sorry, miss," the guard intruded. "Those are the rules."

Cabel peeled my arms from his body, clasped both of my hands in his, and then lowered his head to speak. "I'll be right out here, waiting for you," he promised, his voice nearly a whisper, so the guard couldn't hear. "Okay? I'm not going anywhere. If anything happens..."

"All right," I accepted, understanding my fate. "I'll go."

Breaking contact with Cabel, I let the guard lead me to the door in front of us, very aware of the hammering heart in my chest. When he opened the door, I stepped inside and scanned the stale, white room before me, my eyes darting every which way. Petrified, I pulled a chair out from one of the empty tables and took a seat, woozy with the threat of his nearing presence.

Nervously fidgeting, I folded my hands over the table and squirmed. Then the door clicked open and I withdrew my hands, sliding them beneath my thighs and the seat, as I sat on top of my fingers. Two armed guards escorted a man wearing handcuffs and an orange jumpsuit into the room. The man looked like my father, and yet, he wasn't the man I remembered.

His once youthful locks were now peppered with gray, silver streaking through the last strands of raven black; while his frame remained thin, wiry, his pale skin dry. When he sat down across from me, I felt my legs beginning to shake, my heart pounding so powerfully, that I thought it might explode.

Both prison guards stood against the wall, one on either side of him, but their presence offered no comfort to me. My lungs were on fire, scorching, searing, strangling any ounce of oxygen that was left in me. I didn't think that the chair would be enough to hold me up, to keep my head above water. When he lifted his head and looked into my eyes, it was even harder to breathe.

"Hi Daddy," I rasped.

He narrowed his eyes at me and winced. "What are you doing here?"

Steadying my breathing rate, I exhaled through my nostrils and closed my eyes. I forced myself to think about my mother and the lighthearted way she had graced through life, until he started loving the drink in his hand more than either of us.

"You're sober," I presumed.

"Yes." He nodded so slowly it scared me.

"I don't have many memories of you like that." I wiped my palms on the thighs of my pants, feeling uncomfortable with the sweat. Beads of it were brimming above my upper lip.

"What did you come here for, Finley?" he barked. "To make me feel guilty? To make me confess my sins?"

"No," I swallowed.

His eyes were the color of dark chocolate, turning deeper, until they looked pure black.

"You've gotten taller," he noted, softening, though only for the moment.

"I know. I was ten the last time you saw me."

He chewed at something in his mouth, perhaps a piece of gum. As his eyes pierced through mine without blinking, I stared straight into those windows, the only portal to his black heart and dark soul. I was tired of hurting.

"I came here, because I wanted to see you one last time." Blush spread along the apples of my cheeks, but I didn't let the warmth startle me. "And I thought you might want to see me."

"I don't have anything to tell you, Finley. Go home," he ordered, rising from his seat.

I stood up with him and shouted, "I am home!"

My exclamation froze the man in his tracks, and he sat back down in his chair. I did the same, rooting my elbows to the table, as I folded my hands in the gesture of a prayer.

"I just graduated from college," I began. "I finished a year early, and I'm thinking about applying to grad school. Maybe I could be a psychologist and help people," I paused, "like me."

He levelled his eyes at me and stared, setting his jaw straight. I didn't know where all of this was coming from, because I hadn't even discussed career possibilities with an advisor or with Cabel. But here was the man that I was one-half of, whose blood was running through my veins, whose genes were in my pool, whose eyes were my very own.

"Like you?" he probed.

"Yes," I hissed, for the first time feeling like I was able to keep up.

I could do this. I could face my father, the drinker, the abuser, the murderer, and tell him everything that I had always wanted to, but been too afraid to say, until now.

"You know what you did to me," I snarled, gritting my teeth.

"Children need discipline," he claimed, calm and direct.

"You left bruises. That's not discipline. That's torture."

As a child, I had worn sweaters and jackets year-round, to cover the places where his fingers had left oval-shaped contusions on my arms. For the longest time, the only way I could sleep was on my stomach, because of the painful wounds on my back, where his belt had been. The sting of the leather burned my skin, while the bite of the buckle formed welts.

"What do you want me to do about it?" He lifted his wrists, eyeing the metal cuffs around his hands, as they scraped against the table. "I can't touch you now."

My eyes flickered to the guards against the wall. Both were smoldering, seething, clenching their jaws in frustration. I would have given a million pennies for their thoughts.

"Aren't you scared, Daddy?" I pouted.

"Of what?" He slouched back in the chair, letting his restrained hands fall loosely into his lap.

"Death." I kept my eyes on his, those dark, steady spheres of blackness.

"No." He smiled, and that was how I knew he was lying.

"You don't know how long I've hated you," I revealed, surprised by my own callousness.

"Good," he fired back.

"Good?" I raised my eyebrows at him.

"Yeah," he answered. "What does it matter if you hate me? I'm only your father."

Pressing my lips together, I forced an artificial grin onto my face, because it was the only way to keep me from crying. I should have expected him to say something like that. He had a way of bringing out the worst in himself, because that's all there was.

Finished, I rose from my chair and headed for the door. Our visit was over, since there was nothing left for him to say. He didn't want my forgiveness, and I wasn't about to offer it.

"You're just going to get up and walk away?" he called, yelling after me.

I turned back to him and exhaled. "Yeah," I declared. "I should have a long time ago."

Peace drifted through me, untying the knots in my stomach, settling my frenzied nerves, calming my shaky hands. I felt light, renewed, restored. And when the door shut behind me, and I found Cabel pacing in the hallway, everything finally seemed to make sense.

"What happened?" Cabel asked, anxious as ever.

I adored the ice blue worry in his eyes, because that meant he cared.

"I talked to him," I gushed, feeling like I had just won the lottery.

He held no power over me anymore. My chains had been broken. I was finally free.

"And what did he say?" Cabel brushed his fingers through my hair, tugging a stray lock behind my ear.

"I don't want to talk about it now. Just take me home."

Cabel looked over me protectively and said, "Okay."

A prison guard appeared from around the corner and held out a small paper sack. "Here, he wanted you to have this." When I wouldn't accept the bag, Cabel took it from the guard.

"What is it?" Cabel asked.

"His personal effects, from when we first brought him in. He said that he wanted you to have them," the guard informed, pointing at me.

"I don't want it," I droned. "I don't want anything of his."

"Keep it," he said to Cabel. Then the guard turned on his heel and walked away.

"Come on." Cabel slipped the bag into his pocket, and then wrapped his arm around me. "Let's go home."

Chapter 34

By the time we left the airport, I could hardly keep my eyes open. My entire body felt drained, every muscle, every tendon, every ligament. I felt Cabel unbuckling my seatbelt, as I drifted in and out of consciousness. He picked me up in his arms, curled my legs around his waist, and carried me into the house like a small child.

My head lolled on his shoulder, while my arms dangled over his back. Cabel climbed the staircase and took me into his bedroom, carefully laying me down beneath the covers. I shifted onto my stomach, burrowing my face in the pillow, as Cabel grabbed my ankles, so he could take my shoes off.

Despite my exhaustion, I forced my eyelids open and studied the outline of Cabel in the darkness. He tossed my shoes to the floor, and then tucked me in, pulling the warm sheet over my body. I reached out and touched Cabel's arm, as he gazed down at me with concern.

"Thank you," I mouthed.

Cabel lowered his face and kissed my forehead, then left me to fall asleep and dream.

* * *

When I woke up, Cabel was pacing the floor in front of his empty side of the bed. Squinting my eyes in the daylight, I watched Cabel and yawned. He was still dressed in the same clothes he had been wearing last night, and that paper sack was clasped tightly between his hands.

"Did you go to sleep?" I searched Cabel's tired eyes, his blue irises less crystal than gray. "Have you been up all night?"

"Finley," Cabel called, sitting down on the mattress beside me. He picked a black box out of the paper sack, and then tossed it to the side.

"Yeah?" I replied with worry.

Cabel took my hand and placed the black box in the center of my palm. "I'd ask you today, but I want the time to be right. And I don't want to rush you into anything."

"Cabel, what are you talking about?"

"You should be able to have these now, Finley. They're yours."

Cabel opened the box, revealing my mother's wedding and engagement rings. Taken aback, I sat up in the bed and stared at the golden circles with my mouth ajar. The solitaire diamond glistened beneath me, a family heirloom more than a reminder of my parents' toxic marriage.

My paternal grandfather had given both rings to my grandmother, as their love and shared life together had been a true representation of what I had always wanted, what my parents never had, and what I had been afraid would never come my way.

Silent, I admired the rings, untainted by the memory of my father and what he had done. These were his mother's rings, my mother's rings, my rings, and one day, they would belong to my daughter, who would be showered with more love, more care, more kindness, than my parents had ever shown me.

"You're waiting for the right time?" I confirmed. Cabel nodded, which only made me grin. "Haven't we waited long enough?"

Cabel lifted the side of his mouth into a crooked smirk. "What are you saying?"

I closed the box and dropped it into the palm of his hand.

"I'm saying that if you asked me to marry you today, I would."

"You would?" he wondered, pleasantly surprised.

"Yes." I couldn't hide my smile.

"Are you sure?" Cabel furrowed his brow, worried that he might frighten me away with the prospect of moving too fast.

"Why don't you ask me and you'll find out?" I boldly dared.

For the first time, Cabel's cheeks turned red instead of mine. He settled into the mattress and took my hand in his, then brushed his knuckles along the side of my face. Beaming, I lowered my lashes and sighed, treasuring his touch, his affection, his love. Because I knew that he loved me.

Cabel asked me to marry him, so later that day, I did.

Chapter 35

C abel opened the front door with one hand, while I kept my fingers loosely braided at the nape of his neck. As he carried me over the threshold, I studied his beautiful face and placed a gentle peck on his cheek. Kicking the door closed with his foot, Cabel gently set me down in the foyer, but kept his hand at the small of my back.

My eyes widened in surprise, because the staircase was covered in rose petals. Cabel chuckled at my reaction, then lifted his lips into a teasing smirk. "Go on," he encouraged, releasing me.

A fresh shade of blush tinted my cheeks, as I lifted the skirt of my wedding gown and slowly climbed up the steps. The soft red petals felt comfortable and new beneath my feet, setting the mood for a blissful night of passionate lovemaking. I felt Cabel watching me from down below, while I moved from step to step. Even from a distance, his smoldering looks sent shivers down my spine, as if he had caressed the back of my neck with his hand.

Once I reached the top of the staircase, I

glanced over my shoulder at Cabel and caught him staring from the ground floor. Warmth stirred deep in my belly, expanding and tightening, because I liked the way his eyes glazed over my figure when I wasn't looking.

Following the trail of petals, I walked down the hall and into the master bedroom, where candlelight flickered in the distance. Atop Cabel's dresser, in front of the mirror, sat a gathering of small candles, lined up in the shape of a heart. There was a shiny red apple in the middle of them with the words *Mrs. Jones* carved into the flesh.

My eyes watered at the sight, because Cabel truly was my golden boy.

When his arms encircled my waist, I gazed into the mirror and found Cabel standing behind me with his head on my shoulder. He watched my reflection in the glass, then turned me around to face him, as his darkening eyes wandered the length of my body.

"Finley," he whispered. "Why are you crying?"

I wiped my tears away and sobbed, "Because I'm so happy."

Cabel pressed his forehead to mine, as I felt his hands gliding over my shoulders and arms. The silky white dress felt like heaven, with smooth, satin straps, a beaded bodice, and flowing train. But I wanted nothing more in the world than for Cabel to take it off.

Gentle as ever, Cabel tilted his head to the side and brushed his lush, pouty lips against mine. I responded immediately, craning my neck to keep from eliminating any separation between us. Within seconds, Cabel weaved his fingers through my hair and aligned my body with his, tasting my mouth like he never had before.

Cabel's kisses traveled to the side of my face, as he moved his lips across my cheek, along my jawbone, down my throat, and over my clavicle, before retracing the path he had made. When Cabel blew warm air over the spot beneath my ear, I scraped the back of his neck with my fingernails, and he groaned. Searching for the zipper on my dress, Cabel spun me around and tugged the metal fastener down the length of my spine, his fingertips dancing across my back.

Desperate for his love, I turned to face Cabel and willed him to rip the fabric. Instead, he grasped the satin straps on my dress and pushed them past my shoulders and over my arms, caressing every inch of my skin as he went. Then he tucked his thumbs into either side of the bodice, just beneath my underarms, and pulled the dress down my torso, over my hips and legs, and let the garment fall to the floor.

Leaning forward, I held on to Cabel's back, while he grabbed one ankle at a time and helped me out of my dress. Cabel draped the wedding gown over the wooden footboard at the end of the bed, and then let his eyes scan the length of my body, cloaked in a lacy white slip. I reached my arms out and fiddled with Cabel's tie, until the strip of cloth came loose in my hands. Cabel took the tie from me and tossed it to the ground, so I shoved his jacket off and sent it southward.

Hasty, I unfastened the buttons on Cabel's shirt in a straight, descending line, then untucked the bottom of the shirt from his pants. When I lowered my face and placed a tantalizing kiss between Cabel's pecs, he clutched my chin in the palm of his hand and brought my mouth up to meet his. Cabel took several steps forward, pushing me backwards, until we found the bed.

My body sank into the mattress, as Cabel stretched out beside me, holding my head up to keep his mouth on mine. I twisted his shirtsleeve in my hand and closed my eyes, while Cabel situated his knee between my legs. Panting loudly, I embraced the pulsing, aching warmth that flooded through me and crushed my lips to Cabel's. His sweet breath poured into my mouth, like the fragrance of a ripened fruit, and I moaned.

In an effortless movement, Cabel grabbed my wrist, and then slid his other hand beneath the back of my knee. While I squirmed with tortuous desire, Cabel returned his lips to my throat, before biting my earlobe with his sharp teeth, as I cried out in longing. He clamped his mouth onto mine and silenced me, but I wanted more than sumptuous kisses.

Tired of waiting, I sat up in the bed, ripped Cabel's shirt off his back, and threw it across the room. Cabel pushed my hair over my shoulder, tenderly taking my face between his hands, as he pulled my lips apart with his mouth. I lolled my head back and relaxed, letting Cabel lower my upper body back down to the bed, until I felt the pillow beneath me.

Cabel grasped the hem of my slip, his knuckles tracing over my thighs, light and intoxicating. When he pulled the slip above my arms and chucked it into the pile on the floor, I felt the cool bed sheet against my back, like a chilly ocean breeze. Wasting no time, Cabel kissed the outline of my breasts, as his fingers descended that fine line down the middle of my stomach.

Lost in Cabel's touch, I leaned my head forward to meet his lips and moaned when his bare stomach made contact with mine. Cabel stuck his hands between my back and the mattress, unhooked my bra strap, and then flung the undergarment over his shoulder. I felt my panties slide along my hips, as Cabel tugged them down to my ankles, before I kicked them beneath the covers.

When he reared back and unbuckled his belt, I gnawed at my lip in anticipation. Cabel unzipped his pants and stripped by the bed in front of me, then climbed back on top. My breath was coming out so quickly now, that I felt dizzy, hot blood pulsing loudly in my ears.

Cabel pressed his cheek against the side of my face, and then kissed the tip of my nose. We gazed into each other's eyes, caught up in heat, passion, love, desire, and the unifying gravity that nothing would be the same after this moment. The scent of his cologne surrounded me, engulfing me, cocooning me, but I had always liked that smell.

With no warning, Cabel parted his lips over my jaw, as I turned my head to the side and gasped. Cabel stilled above me, holding himself up with his arms on either side of my face.

"Are you okay?"

"Yeah," I panted. "I'm fine. Just kiss me."

Cabel obeyed at once, molding his lips to mine, as I dug my nails into his back.

At first, it felt like I was drowning, but couldn't bear to take a breath of oxygen. Then the sensation changed, and it felt like I was falling straight through the clouds, dropping deep into the darkest ocean, but didn't want to stop. Of all the many pleasures in life, this one was the greatest.

Chapter 36

The next morning, I woke up tangled in a mess of bed sheets, with Cabel's leg sandwiched between both of mine. Once he realized that I was awake, Cabel splayed his fingers along my ribcage and pressed his lips beneath my ear.

"Good morning," he whispered.

I rolled onto my side to face him and gazed into his icy blue eyes. They held new meaning now, as he smoldered, playfully smiling back at me.

"How do you feel?" He tucked a loose strand of hair behind my ear, and then traced my lips with his thumb. They still felt tender from last night.

"Sore. Tired. Hungry," I prattled.

Cabel chuckled darkly, resting his head in the palm of his hand, as he sat up on his elbow.

"Let me spoil you," he tempted, gifting sweet kisses on my neck.

"Okay," I sighed, unraveling with pleasure.

Cabel laughed into my neck, his freshly grown stubble rough and sharp.

"Where do you want to go for our honeymoon?"

His hot breath warmed my flesh, turning my cheeks bright red. Feeling brave, I rose up and climbed on top of him, my knees at either side of his waist. Cabel put his hands on my bare thighs, while I leaned over him and placed my lips to his ear.

"I thought we were already on it," I remarked.

Cabel's fingers trailed my hips, up to my waist, and then landed on either side of my face.

"Well," he snickered, "you aren't too hard to please."

Grinning, I fixed my mouth on Cabel's perfect lips, relishing the feel of his hands twisting through my hair. When I pulled away, he groaned, but the feral sound made me giggle. With the sheet wrapped around my naked body, I hopped down from the bed and waltzed over to the dresser. All of the candles had burned out, but the apple at the center of them remained.

Ravenous, I plucked the fruit up with my hand, and then dropped down to my knees, searching Cabel's pants on the floor. I found a small pocket knife and rejoiced.

"What are you doing?" Cabel wondered, amused by my behavior.

"Aren't you hungry?"

I strolled back over to the bed and sat down beside Cabel, offering him the apple. His frosty blue eyes glistened, as he read the front peel, where *Mrs. Jones* remained carved in perfectly scripted lettering. When I opened the pocket knife and pressed the blade against the center of the fruit, Cabel grabbed my wrist.

"Wait," he paused, "you want to eat it?"

"Why wouldn't we?" I questioned.

Cabel looked down at the apple, most likely reflecting on all of the other apples we had shared, and their hidden, illicit meaning at the time.

"I don't know." Cabel opened his eyes, as light washed over his face. His smile was too beautiful for plain old words to describe.

I cut a small chunk from the apple, then handed it to Cabel. His fingertips brushed over the center of my palm, as he took the piece of fruit from me.

"There's no point in wasting it," I continued.

Cabel watched me reduce the apple to five equal slices, looking on with intrigue and desire. We shared the fruit in silence, eating our respective slices. But then a strange, mind-rattling thought pervaded all others, and I couldn't ignore the anxiety. Perhaps this was what it was like to taste forbidden fruit, when the fruit was no longer forbidden.

"Are we crazy?" I wondered.

"What do you mean?" Confusion altered Cabel's features, as he chewed the last bit of apple.

"For getting married so fast. I mean, who does that?"

Cabel looked into my eyes and scowled.

"Finley, what are you saying?"

"I'm not saying anything," I snapped, biting back louder than I had intended.

"Yes, you are," he hissed.

"Just forget it, Cabel." I took a breath and let my head fall into the pillow.

"Are you having second thoughts?"

"Ugh! About what?"

"About marrying me!" he yelled.

"Why are you so angry?"

"You brought this up!"

"Cabel-"

"You regret it, don't you? You regret marrying me?"

"Cabel," I scolded, hardly believing his sudden outburst.

"I knew it," he said. "I knew you wouldn't stay with me."

Cabel peeled the sheet back and trudged into the closet, where he got dressed in a hurry, stepping out fully clothed within seconds.

"Cabel," I whined. "Where are you going?"

"I need to think." Cabel walked out the door, leaving me naked in his bed.

Frantic, I held the sheet around me and chased him down the hallway. "Cabel, wait!" I cried, nearly tripping over my own two feet. "Don't leave me!"

"Why?" Cabel stopped at the top of the staircase, while I clung to his arm. "Because you love me or because you don't want to be alone?"

His cold words crashed down on me like a bucket of ice, compelling me to release him from my grip. Cabel turned away with his jaw clenched, perhaps realizing the coldness of his words. I watched him barrel down the steps, and then slam the front door behind him on his way out.

I collapsed on the staircase with no more than the bed sheet to comfort me. I must have sat there for hours with tears in my eyes, wondering how the fire could have so quickly turned to ice.

Chapter 37

When Cabel returned, I was lying in his four-poster bed, still donning the sheet that I had been tangled in earlier. Hearing the front door open, I scurried into the closet and stepped into a pair of jeans, then threw a loose t-shirt over my head. I hadn't eaten anything since that apple.

I found Cabel downstairs in the kitchen, with his back turned to me. Bags of groceries filled up all of the counter space, as I realized that the only place he had been was the store. At first, I didn't want to alert him of my presence, because that seemed to be the equivalent of waking a sleeping dragon. But then I couldn't stand to be near him and not speak, so I opened my mouth.

"Hi," was all I managed to get out.

Cabel froze, as I noticed the way his neck stiffened in response. He placed a handful of canned vegetables in the cupboard overhead, then opened the fridge, where he slammed a carton of milk onto the top shelf. When he wouldn't stop ignoring me, I furrowed my brow in frustration.

"Aren't you going to say something?" I

demanded.

Cabel walked straight past me, leaving the rest of the groceries unattended. Relentless, I followed him down the hallway, into the foyer, and up the staircase. When he walked into the master bedroom without so much as looking at me, I kept at his heels.

"Cabel, we need to talk," I insisted, tugging his elbow. Cabel turned around and exhaled, his eyes downcast, as he crossed his arms over his chest. He may have started out as my professor, but Cabel Jones was my husband now, and he was going to speak to me.

"About what?" he growled.

"About us," I cried. "I don't understand what happened. What did I do wrong?"

"Why did you marry me, Finley?"

"What?" I reacted, my breath shaky, as he glared down at me.

"You never said you loved me," he accused. "Not since we've been back together."

"Yes, I have," I argued.

In the past three days, I hadn't paid much attention to every word coming out of my mouth or every word that hadn't. Everything had been such a blur. I was his girlfriend one day, his fiancé the next, and now I was his wife. We were the walking definition of a whirlwind engagement.

"Don't lie," he commanded. "You're not very good at it."

"Cabel, I'm sorry. Just because I haven't told

you that I love you, doesn't mean that I don't," I reasoned, but Cabel glanced away regardless. I grabbed his chin and pulled his face down to mine, tired of being ignored. "I do love you, and I wouldn't have married you if I didn't. You're the only man I've ever loved and the only man I ever will."

Withdrawing my hand, I rocked back on my heels and slipped my hands into the back pockets of my jeans. Cabel searched my face with a pair of guarded, questioning looks. I couldn't take the criticism anymore, so I fled, out of the bedroom, down the staircase, through the hallway, and into the kitchen. Now Cabel could see what it felt like to be ignored.

"Finley," Cabel called, his tone more whiney than apologetic. I felt his presence lurking behind me, while I put the rest of the groceries away. "Finley, I'm sorry."

When Cabel touched the back of my neck with his hand, I turned away from him to store the cereal boxes in the pantry. Cabel groaned aloud, not liking the same dose of coldness that he had just given me. I hoped that the feeling stung as much as his words had stung me.

The phone rang, but I kept myself distracted, gathering up all of the grocery bags and stuffing them at the bottom of the pantry. Cabel stalked towards the phone on the wall and answered it.

"Hello?" he grumbled.

I shut the pantry door, returned to the sink,

and filled a glass with tap water.

"Oh..." Cabel's voice dropped, as I felt an ominous force coming through the phone line. "Finley?" He covered the receiver of the phone with his hand, while I glanced across the kitchen at him in terror. "I'm sorry, but your father, he's-"

The glass of water fell from my hand, shattering across the kitchen floor. I hurried out of the room and ran back up the staircase, until I had locked myself inside the master bathroom. All these years, I had convinced myself that I wanted him to die, that he deserved to die, that he needed to die, for my mother's sake. But all I felt was guilty.

Shaking, I turned the faucet on and watched the tub fill up with warm water. I never thought I would cry. I had always known that there were no tears left for him. And yet, here I was, weeping uncontrollably on the bathroom floor, because he was gone.

"Finley!" Cabel stood outside the bathroom door, twisting the handle with fury. "Let me in! Please!" he begged.

I sat down in the bathtub, not bothering to take off my clothes, or pay attention to the rising water level. All I could do was be still, with my head against the tile wall behind me.

"Finley! Open the door!" Cabel yelled, banging his fist against the wood. "Look, I'm sorry about leaving today and yelling at you. But please," he lamented, "don't lock me out."

Burying my face in my hands, I let the water rise to the surface, and then spill over the edges. Cabel broke the lock on the door and forced it open, only to find me trembling at the center of the tub. He rushed inside the bathroom, turned the water off, and pushed my dampened locks out of my face, his eyes flooding with worry at my appearance.

"Oh baby," he crooned. "I'm sorry. I'm so, so sorry."

Cabel took off his shoes, and then sat down in the tub beside me. When he reached out to pull me into his arms, I let him, as he cradled my head against his chest. Gentle as ever, Cabel ran his fingers through my hair, letting me weep, letting me suffer, letting me mourn.

When the water turned cold and I had no tears left to cry, Cabel lifted my face in his hands. Swallowing, I gazed up at him with longing and want. His fingertips brushed across the surface of my skin so carefully, so smoothly, so kindly.

I looked up with a pair of pleading eyes, and whimpered, "Make love to me."

Cabel rubbed his thumb across my cheek, and then brought his mouth to mine. I parted my lips slowly at first, taking my time, as I sat up, sliding my knees on either side of his lap. Cabel placed his hands along my waistline, while I scraped my teeth along the edge of his earlobe. He moaned in pleasure, slipping his fingers beneath my shirt, then lifting it over my head.

Seductive, I burrowed my nails into Cabel's neck and molded my mouth to his, taking control of the kiss. When he picked at the hem of his shirt, my hands skimmed over his stomach, and we took the garment off together. Biting my lip, I searched his lovely, endearing eyes, at the same time he was searching mine. Cabel kneaded the bare skin of my back, just above the waistband on my jeans, while I rested my hands on his shoulders and sat down between his legs in the water.

Knotting my fingers through Cabel's hair, I sank into each and every kiss and curled myself around his hips. When I felt his tongue at the edge of my teeth, Cabel squeezed my body and pulled me closer. "I've never wanted anyone as badly as I want you," he rasped.

Our mouths crashed into each other's, as I gladly let Cabel claim me for well into the night.

Chapter 38

In the middle of the night, I heard something crash downstairs, perhaps a broken glass. Startling awake, I reached for Cabel beside me in the bed, but he was gone.

Groggy, I smoothed my hand over my face and swung my legs over the side of the mattress. My feet planted into the soft carpet, as I treaded across the floor and into the closet. I snatched my satin robe off its hanger and slipped my arms through the sleeves, then tied the sash around my waist and yawned.

Lazily making my way down the staircase, I held on to the banister and listened for the sounds I had heard earlier. The silent foyer haunted my spirit, because I could sense that something wasn't quite right. When I turned down the corridor and found Cabel alone in the dark living room, gazing out the moonlit window with his back to me, the tension in my body dissipated, and I breathed a sigh of relief.

"Couldn't sleep?" I guessed, approaching his shirtless figure.

Cabel wore a pair of long sweatpants, the cuffs

hanging over his bare feet. He stood terrifyingly still, like a statue.

I took a step closer and swallowed. "Cabel?"

He ignored me, then lifted his hand, and I heard the clink of ice cubes in the glass he was holding. Cabel pressed his lips to the rim, sucking down the last of the amber liquid. At that moment, I spotted the whiskey bottle in his other hand, only illuminated by the glow of the moonlight.

My golden boy was gone.

"Cabel," I gasped, wholly crushed and betrayed.

I never should have married him so quickly. We had once known each other, but that didn't mean that we did anymore. Two years had left me lonely and exhausted, but the time had produced a different effect on Cabel.

"What are you doing?"

Cabel cocked his head back and acknowledged my presence in the room. He retreated from the window, set the glass and bottle down on the coffee table, and then shoved past me. I gritted my teeth in frustration, feeling a boiling hot rage surfacing from within.

Livid, I stormed after Cabel and snatched his arm, jerking him back to me. "You're drinking now?" I accused, gladly letting the anger consume me.

"I just needed to relax," he mumbled, wiping the back of his hand across his mouth.

Cabel smelled sweet. Cabel smelled pungent.

Cabel smelled like my father.

"Relax?" I echoed. "I thought you were relaxed," I conveyed, recalling our earlier encounter in the bathtub and our tangling of the bed sheets immediately afterwards. "Why am I not enough?"

Cabel withdrew from me and stepped into the corridor, on his way to the foyer. Trailing his footsteps, I sped in front of Cabel and confronted him at the bottom of the staircase. He held his hands behind his back and chuckled, mocking me.

"Why would you do this to me?" I stood on the fifth step, so I would be taller than Cabel. "You know how I feel about alcohol! You know how I feel about drinking!"

"It was only one glass," he belittled, flattening his hands over my shoulders.

I stared into his eyes and scowled. "Then why was the whole bottle empty?"

Cabel cupped my cheek in his hand, but I revolted, pushing him away from me, as I turned to climb the steps.

It was over. We were done. I couldn't believe that I had been so stupid, but I wasn't going to make my mother's mistake. Tomorrow, I would find an attorney who could draw up the quickest annulment papers, and then sign on the dotted line.

Near the top of the staircase, Cabel grabbed my arm and spun me around to face him. Before I could react, his hands were painfully rooted to my waist, and his tongue forced its way into my mouth, sloppy and wet. Fighting against him, I bucked and screamed, frightened of the man who had become my husband.

When Cabel broke off the kiss, only so he could breathe, I raised my hand and slapped him across the side of his face as hard as I could. Cabel froze before me, while I swallowed, panting loudly in front of him. Astonished, he removed his hooks from my side and let me go.

Still catching my breath, I turned my back to him and rubbed the palm of my hand that I had slapped him with. It stung from the contact with his skin, and I was surprised by how much that hurt. Just as I reached the second floor, Cabel pulled me back and tossed me down the staircase.

Screaming in terror, I tumbled down the steps, feeling every stiff corner beat against my back, my knees, my stomach. When I landed on the hardwood floor, black dots floated over my eyes. Cabel glided down the steps and hovered over me, his feet by my face. But then I heard him unbuckle his belt, and I couldn't help shrieking in horror.

"NOOOO!" I wailed, as he knelt down and clamped his hand around my wrist.

"Finley," a different voice said, deep and ghastly.

All of the blood drained from my body, because that voice sent bile up my throat and into my mouth. My bones turned to mush, no need to break them. I was already broken.

"I told you not to leave the milk on the counter," he growled. "Maybe this time you'll remember."

Even in the darkness, I could make out the pure blacks of his brown eyes. I could have spotted them a mile away, because everything in them told me to run.

"NOOOO!" I screamed, as he raised the belt over his head.

"Finley!"

I felt hands on my shoulders, shaking me, rousing me, waking me.

"Finley!"

My eyelids slammed open, as I jolted upright in the bed, a sleek sheen of sweat coating my body. Cabel turned on the lamp by the bed and stared down at me, his eyes darting in confusion, worry, and fear.

"Finley, are you okay?" He brushed the fallen hair out of my eyes and loudly exhaled.

"I feel sick," I whispered.

Shaking, I leapt out of the bed and ran into the bathroom. I tried sitting on the edge of the tub with my head between my legs. When it felt like I could breathe again, I held my hands over my thighs and looked up. Cabel was standing in the doorway.

"Do I need to take you to the doctor?"

"No," I breathed. "I'm fine. I'll be all right."

Cabel approached me, kneeling down on the

tile floor. I shut my eyes and inhaled through my nostrils. When Cabel touched my hand, I flinched, opening my eyes wide. I saw the pain in his eyes.

"Are they always this bad?" The skin surrounding his eyes crinkled with concern.

"Sometimes," I admitted.

My dreams were always terrifying, though tonight had been an anomaly. Unfortunately, the nightmares were real, because I had already lived them. The nightmares were memories.

"Will they ever go away?" My voice sounded small, and Cabel was too afraid to touch me.

I wanted to cry.

"No," Cabel said. "But neither will I."

Sobbing aloud, I pulled Cabel into my arms and clung to him more tightly than I ever had before. Cabel consoled me gently, rubbing my back, stroking my hair, kissing my face. When he threaded his fingers through my hair and gazed into my eyes, I knew that I wanted nothing more than to taste his lips, to touch his skin, to feel his heart beating against mine.

"I don't want to hate him anymore," I confessed.

Those were the words that I never thought I would say.

Cabel exhaled with a small smile. "Then don't."

Somehow, he had a way of making me believe that everything was going to be all right.

Cabel brought my mouth to his, as I whimpered in delight, folding my legs around his hips. With his hands beneath my shirt, Cabel stood up and took me with him, slowly walking into the bedroom, where he crawled onto the mattress and laid me down beneath him.

Chapter 39

The next day felt like the closest thing to normal that I had experienced in a long time. Cabel helped me pack up boxes, as we began the arduous process of moving the rest of my belongings into his house. It almost felt surreal, the fact that he would be lying beside me every night, an infinite number of sleepovers, an ongoing marathon of slumber parties with the man I loved.

Looking back on the last night we had spent together in my apartment, I remembered how heartbroken I had felt, understanding that Cabel would never be anything more than my professor. But now, I realized that those two years spent apart were the best thing that could have ever happened to us, because I valued his presence that much more.

When we returned to the house, Cabel and I sat on the kitchen counter, eating peanut butter and banana sandwiches like a pair of eight-year-olds. My legs dangled over the edge, while I eyed Cabel across from me and smiled. Maybe love didn't have to be so complicated, after all.

"Cabel?" I set the rest of my sandwich down

on a paper plate and crossed my arms over my chest.

"Hmm?" He took a sip of milk from his glass, and then gave me his full attention.

"I think I want to go to grad school. Not to teach, but to become a psychologist. What do you think?" I chirped, gripping the edge of the counter with my hands.

"Well, you need to set up a time to take the GRE. You'll need to request your transcripts to be sent over as well. Fill out the applications, but make sure you get some letters of recommendation from your undergrad professors."

My eyes widened with excitement, as I leaned forward, beaming at him.

"I'm pretty sure mine wouldn't count," he chuckled.

I nodded, absorbing all of the information, while nibbling on a corner of my sandwich.

"You'll need to get your Ph.D. to become a psychologist."

"Then we'll both be doctors."

"It could take up to five years," he warned.

"It didn't take you that long." I licked a drop of peanut butter off my thumb and smiled.

"No."

"I just graduated a year early," I noted. "So why wouldn't I do grad school the same way? You've been on the fast track, and so have I. It might only take me two to three years instead of five."

"Just think about it first, Finley. That's all I'm saying. Grad school's a big commitment."

"Okay," I chimed.

Sliding down from the kitchen counter, I leaned up on the tips of my toes and kissed Cabel on the mouth. When I pulled away, Cabel set his hands at the small of my back and reeled me into his embrace.

"No," Cabel protested, touching his nose against mine.

I grabbed his biceps to steady my balance, and then closed my eyes. As he molded his mouth to mine, that familiar electric current sent shock waves through my body, stirring my soul, awakening my skin, and solidifying the tender affection in my heart.

I knew that I would never love another man the way I loved Cabel Jones.

Chapter 40

Later that afternoon, Cabel returned from the post office and tossed the mail onto the bed. Yawning, I sat up and pressed my hands into the mattress, still dressed in Cabel's shirt. Now I understood why married couples took so many naps.

I needed to rest; it was the only way to keep up.

"What's this?" I asked, tugging a large manila envelope loose from the pile.

"Who cares?" Cabel curled up beside me and planted a string of kisses along my neck, kicking the rest of the mail off the bed.

Furrowing my brow, I held up the envelope and read the names written on the recipient line.

Mr. & Mrs. Cabel Jones

"That's weird," I spoke under my breath. "We haven't even been married a week."

Cabel grabbed my legs and pulled me onto the flat of my back, so my head slid from the headboard to the pillow. I yelped in surprise, because Cabel didn't usually move so fast. His hands fiddled with the hem of the shirt around me, tickling my sensitive skin.

"Cabel, stop," I giggled. "Wait a minute."

He rocked back onto his heels in disappointment, his knees already positioned at my hips. The look on his face made me laugh, because he couldn't stand the minimal space between us.

"Look at this," I urged, showing him the envelope.

Cabel groaned, then rolled onto his back and sat up beside me.

"It's addressed to both of us, but I haven't even told anyone that we got married yet. Did you?"

"No."

Cabel opened the flap on the envelope and reached inside. What he found was a stack of photographs that turned my blood cold. They were pictures of me and Cabel in the cabin, and we weren't wearing many clothes.

"Cabel," I breathed, my face frozen in shock, as he flipped through the photos.

Two years ago, someone had been watching us in the forest.

I remembered that night in the cabin vividly, when Cabel had been the ice to my fire. I could still feel sweat trickling down my spine, at the memory of how hot I had been. If not for Cabel's cool touch, I might not have been able to make it through the night.

But the pictures told a different story, revealing shots of Cabel taking his clothes off and then removing mine. The image of his fingers in the waistband of my pants made me feel queasy, until I saw the last photo. Gaping, I turned to Cabel with a questioning, confusing look of unawareness.

Before I could ask, Cabel gathered up the photographs in his arms, along with the envelope, and stormed out of the room. Fearfully lost, I got out of the bed and followed his quick footsteps, eventually landing downstairs, in the kitchen by the sink. Cabel slapped the pictures down on the counter, and then rifled through the drawers until he found a lighter.

"Cabel, what's going on?" I panicked. "Who took those pictures?"

"I don't know," he droned, his head down.

"But that was back when-"

"You think I don't know that already?" Cabel snarled.

All of the photos were dated at the bottom.

When I had still been a student.

Cabel's student.

"What are we going to do? Who all knows about us? About us back then?"

"I don't know!" Cabel snapped. He flicked the spark wheel with his thumb, but the lighter produced no flame. Frustrated, Cabel slid the lighter across the counter and walked over to the pantry, where he found a box of matches.

"What if the school finds out?" I kept at Cabel's heels, despite the fact that his mind was elsewhere. "You could lose your job, your career, everything you've worked for," I stressed.

Cabel struck a match against the side of the box, and a glowing yellow flame produced. He dropped the photos into the sink and touched the flame to the edge of the paper.

"I never should have married you so soon after graduation," I worried, pacing the kitchen floor. "They'll figure it out. They'll know what we did."

The photos blackened and withered beneath the growing flame, while Cabel remained focused on the task at hand. Guilt rushed over me, because I had been the one to lead him astray. I had been the one to help him break the rules, forget his place, and cross that forbidden line.

"You were worth every risk," Cabel uttered, his face aglow from the fire.

Frozen in place, I glanced down at the burning photographs, while tears brimmed over the surface of my eyes. The last picture sat atop the stack of flaming photos, the fire closing in on the image of our embracing bodies at the center. I had never known that Cabel had cared that night, back when we hardly knew each other, when we had to run, when we had to hide.

In a brief moment of forbidden affection, Cabel had done what no professor should. Tears blurred my vision, as the shrinking photograph taunted me, because the scene was exactly what it looked like. I stumbled out of the kitchen and cried, leaving Cabel to turn the memory to ash.

While all of the pictures were incriminating, I

saw no possible way of innocently explaining the last. I had been boiling over with a fever, and Cabel wouldn't stop shivering. We had been forced to huddle together beneath the covers, merely to survive the night. But what Cabel had done sealed our fates together in a way that would leave us eternally bound to one another.

When I calmed down enough to return to the kitchen, Cabel hunched his shoulders forward and leaned into the sink. The last of the flames danced across his crystal blue eyes, a striking reflection of fire in a pool of ice. I pressed the small of my back into the counter and stared at the floor beneath me, wondering how we ever could have thought that we wouldn't get caught.

Cabel walked away and left the last picture smoldering in the sink. My eyes followed his figure, as he drifted out of the room and into the hallway. I heard his fading footsteps, until nothing remained but the sound of burning paper. Approaching the sink, I flicked my eyes down, though the photo was nearly gone. Only our faces and torsos remained, while the fire kept on consuming.

I knew that the image would come back to haunt us.

I knew that Cabel would take the blame.

I knew that I didn't want him to.

In the photo, that last picture of us, the one that tied Cabel's hands and made my own perspire with sweat, Cabel had done something that was as familiar to me now as breathing. Cabel had bestowed his secret affection upon me, while I was sleeping soundly beside him.

Cabel Jones had kissed me.

Tell Me Your Favorite Part!

If you enjoyed Me & Mr. Jones, I invite you to head over to Amazon and let me know your favorite part. Reviews are so important to an author's career, because they help new readers like you discover the book. Even if you didn't enjoy Me & Mr. Jones, I'd still love it if you could take three minutes to let me know what you think of the book.

Leaving a review is super easy:

1) Go to Me & Mr. Jones Book Page on Amazon

2) Scroll Down and click "Write a Customer Review"

3) Sign in to Amazon if prompted

4) Select a star rating

5) Write a few short words (or long words, I won't judge)

6) Click the 'submit' button

I thank you in advance!

Acknowledgements

As always, ample gratitude goes out to my family and friends, who have been graciously supportive and encouraging throughout this journey. Thank you for your patience and understanding.

Also, a huge shout-out to my newfound acquaintances out there in the book blogging world. I am especially indebted to Larissa at *The Howling Turtle*, Naylene at *More than Scribbles*, and Aly at *Reading Shy with Aly* for shining a light on *Emerald Green*. Thank you all for the promotional pieces, interviews, and guest posts. You girls are awesome.

Lastly, to the reader. Thank you for taking the time to lose yourself among the pages of this novel. Finley and Cabel are like family to me, and I feel extremely blessed to share their story with you. I hope you have enjoyed their company as much as I have.

About the Author

Lindsay Marie Miller was born and raised in Tallahassee, Florida, where she graduated from high school as Valedictorian. At sixteen, she started writing her first novel, *Emerald Green*, after being inspired by Stephenie Meyer's International Bestselling *Twilight Saga*. During her time in college, Lindsay wrote 5 more novels and over 100 songs. After graduating Summa Cum Laude from Florida State University, she put her B.A. in English Literature to good use and published her debut novel, *Emerald Green*. An author of over 10 Romance Titles, Lindsay currently resides in her hometown of Tallahassee where she is always working on her next novel.

To learn more, please visit:

www.lindsaymariemillerauthor.com

Sign up for Lindsay's newsletter:

lindsaymariemillerauthor.com/claim-your-free-book/

Join Lindsay on Facebook at:

facebook.com/LindsayMarieMillerAuthor

Follow Lindsay on Twitter at:

twitter.com/Lindsay_MMiller

LOOK FOR THE NEXT BOOK

AVAILABLE NOW

Praise for *ME & MR. JONES*

"A Suspenseful, Fast Paced and Utterly Brilliant Read!"

—Amazon Reviewer

"Left me with a massive book hangover!"

— A Book Lover's Emporium

"A fast paced, quick read that will hook you on this series."

—A One-Click Addict's Book Blog

"Not your typical forbidden fruit story."

—Amazon Reviewer

"...totally blew my mind."

—Kylie's Fiction Addiction

"Hot, sexy... Loved it."

—Amazon Reviewer

DON'T MISS THESE OTHER BOOKS BY
LINDSAY MARIE MILLER

The Girl in the Woods

Emerald Green

Honey Gold

Mr. Jones & Me

Jungle Eyes

Island Smile

Coastal Spirit

Single

An Arrangement

An Accident

Mercy

AND LOOK FOR HER NEW NOVEL

Available in January 2018